SIGHTS ON THE SEAL

ALEXIS ABBOTT

PATHFORGERS PUBLISHING

Get an EXCLUSIVE book, **FREE** just as a thank you for signing up for my newsletter! Plus you'll never miss a new release, cover reveal, or promotion!

http://alexisabbott.com/newsletter

I am still numb with shock. Utterly paralyzed with disbelief.

I never, ever expected to hear from him again. When my cell phone rang earlier while I was in the bathtub, it was only by sheer luck of circumstance that I sighed and stepped out of the thick, comforting warmth of the bathroom to answer the call. And only because I was expecting someone to call — someone very important and very needy. You see, the client I am working for on this particular gig owns an extremely powerful, far-reaching business enterprise, with its headquarters in the city of Mississauga, Ontario. That's why I'm here in this ritzy hotel the likes of which I would never book for myself on my own dime, even though I make pretty decent money as a private contract security specialist. I possess a staggering level of security clearance after holding a high position in the Canadian sector of NATO years ago, which I have used to my advantage now that I'm a freelancer.

My client, a rather trembly and pale older man named Mr. Green who wears oversized suits even though he could certainly afford a private tailor, is quite nervous about protecting his assets. During my week-long stay here in Mississauga, he has called me no less than forty-eight times with various questions and concerns, even though he has seen me in person every single day. He's stomped all over my patience, with his patent-leather boot hovering just over my very last nerve. But he's given me a high-profile, extremely well-paying job here, so as much as I want to ignore him or tell him to calm down and take his jitters elsewhere, I have no choice but to answer his calls — every, single one of them.

Earlier this evening I had just began to ease my aching, naked body into the steaming water when I heard the tell-tale *brrrring* of my cell phone ring tone. With a frustrated groan I stepped out of the shower to dry my hands on a fluffy white hotel towel and slide the screen open to answer the call.

But I hesitated when I noticed that my client's name was not illuminated on the screen. No, it was a number I didn't recognize at all, and I squinted at the series of numbers intently, wracking my brain for any memory of such a sequence. But nothing came to mind. Still, there was a good chance that it could be another potential client calling after being referred to me by some pleased former customer of mine. And with the situation I was dealing with back home... well, I was in no position to turn down a potential gig.

So I took a deep breath and answered the call with a curt, businesslike greeting of, "Hello, you have reached Summers Private Security, this is Rebecca."

There was a pause. I waited impatiently for someone to speak on the other end of the line, as I was more than eager to get back in my steamy tub instead of continuing to stand here shivering nakedly on the phone with this mystery stranger.

"Hello?" I repeated. "Is anyone there?"

And the voice that finally spoke, filling my ears with deep, velvety thrums of familiarity, both flooded me with warmth and raised goosebumps on my flesh at the same time.

"Becca," said a male voice, and he spoke the two simple syllables of my name like they formed a reverent prayer. Like my name was some magical incantation and he had been holding the powerful sounds of it between his lips for ages, just waiting to expel them out into the air once more.

I recognized his voice instantly. Without a doubt. Without a second thought. And just like that, I was transported backwards, punched in the gut so hard that I was repelled into the past. Suddenly, it was like I could nearly smell the residual musk of collective body odor, gunpowder, diesel fuel, and the unmistakable but indescribable smell of the blisteringly hot desert. The symphony of ominous scents that formed the eau de parfum of my time in Afghanistan as a NATO officer, surrounded by exhausted, war-beaten men and women of many nationalities to whom I delivered goods and relief as much as I could.

I was thrust back into the moment I first looked across a crowded open air market, over the carts of produce and vendors selling t-shirts and fabrics, to lock eyes with the most handsome and intimidating man I had ever seen in person.

My mind spiraled straight back to the night in my private tent, our bodies moving against one another in the heat of my little temporary home while the air cooled outside. Nighttime in the desert was surprisingly cold, a sharp contrast to the miserable heat of the daylight hours. But the two of us, one Canadian, one American, both a little lost and lustful, pressed together to form our own campfire, striking powerful sparks between our undulating bodies.

It was him.

"Adrian," I breathed, my fingertips going cold as I clutched the phone to my ear, desperate not to lose signal, desperate to keep the soft comfort of his voice coming through the receiver as long as I could possibly manage.

"Yeah, it's me," he replied, and I felt my knees start to buckle as my stomach twisted into knots.

"How did you — what are you — where are you calling from?" I stammered, struggling to even find the words to say. Nothing seemed appropriate. No sequence of words I could string together would possibly convey the complicated storm of emotions I was feeling at the sound of his voice in my ear. I heard him sigh, and a shiver ran down my spine.

"I just landed in Toronto. My tour is over and I… I needed to find you, Becca. Wherever you are. I don't know where you live or where you've been all this time, but I remembered that you were from Canada and you wanted to go home. I need to see you. I need to hold you in my arms. I don't care how far I have to go, if I have to fly halfway around the world or walk a thousand miles on foot. I will go to you, Rebecca. I just have to," Adrian explained.

He was in Toronto.

Just a few miles north of where I was. He was so close. I trembled, nearly panting with exhilaration, with mingled joy and horror to find out that he was here. I had never imagined that I would see him ever again. All this time, these two long, life-changing years, I simply assumed he was a figure to remain shrouded in the mists of my past. A broad-shouldered, hulking silhouette I sometimes looked back to when I felt lonely and afraid.

But now, he was here. Nearly within reach.

"Becca?" he prompted, and I realized I still needed to answer him. So I did.

"I'm here. I'm in Mississauga. You're nearly on my doorstep," I responded breathlessly. "The-the Arcadian. Room 605."

"I'll be there soon," Adrian said, and with that, he hung up.

And now I'm standing here in the bathroom again, letting the hot water drip down over my shoulders, thick beads of water rolling over my full breasts, sliding down my smooth back and bum. I'm supposed to be washing my hair, but I keep getting distracted as my mind wanders repeatedly back to Adrian. I have not seen or heard from him in two years, ever since his work as a Navy SEAL stole him away from the camp where I was stationed, but he still plays a starring role in all of my wildest, hottest fantasies. He is still the one whose body my own longs for, the man who walks tall and strong in my sweetest dreams. He is the man I lust for, even now. Even though we were only intimate one time, on that fateful night in the desert.

Both of us were so raw and passionate that night after fighting our magnetic attraction for over a week at the camp. We were both there on duty, with enormous responsibilities weighing down our shoulders, and there was no room or time for some romantic dalliance. Still, that level of animalistic lust could not be shelved. It could not be ignored. And so we fell into each other's arms with a unifying sigh of relief and ultimately, of release. We were not careful. We were not slow.

It was fast and hard and everything the two of us needed so badly in the moment.

It was a distraction from the bleakness of our surroundings and the perils that haunted our every step out there in the desert. It was a momentary lapse in attention and vigilance, a break from our usually upstanding attention to duty.

And it was the night that altered the course of my life forever.

I shiver, even under the warm water. I can't believe this is happening. He's coming back for me.

Just like I imagined he would a thousand times before, making up these impossible scenarios in my head. I have pictured him striding confidently back into my life, his handsome face bright and bronzed from the desert sun like it was in my still-vivid memories, his enormous height and finely-honed muscles striking awe and desire within me once again.

I close my eyes and let my hand wander down between my thighs, softly stroking that sweet, tanta-lizing slit, slick with the memory of Adrian's powerful body moving against mine in the desert. My lips slide open in a quiet sigh as I stroke myself, my other hand coming up to caress my breast, my stiffening nipple. A spiral of delicious sensation moves downward through me as I rock my hips forward and backward, rutting into the rhythmic pressure of my own fingertips between my legs.

Then, suddenly, I force myself to stop. I don't have time. What am I doing standing here in the bathroom touching myself to the thought of Adrian when the real thing is going to appear at my door in less than thirty minutes? I know it's only a short drive from the Toronto airport to my hotel, if the cab ride I took is any indication of measurement. And as commanding and charismatic as Adrian is, I'm sure it takes him barely a split second to get a taxi to stop for him. But then I remember his words from so long ago, when he insisted upon getting a vehicle for us rather than just paying a local driver:

"In my line of work, I have learned not to trust anyone but myself. Especially behind the wheel. I need to be in control. Nobody can take me anywhere I don't want to go. It may sound unreasonable, but this is the way I have to do things," he told me, shrugging.

Yes. Of course he will rent his own car. But even that will only take him a few minutes of fussing with the rental services at the airport. I don't have time for anything. Unless I want him to show up and find me naked and dripping, with wet hair and no makeup on.

It will be our first reunion in two years, and much has changed since then. Of course, he saw me without makeup, with my then-shoulder length dark hair tied back in a utilitarian ponytail, all the time when we served together. In Afghanistan, I was only there to work. It didn't matter if I was pretty or even decently presentable, as long as I was properly dressed, alert, and ready to follow orders.

But now, I don't want him to see me that way. I've changed… in more ways than I could have ever imagined back when we first met. I am a different person now, with totally different priorities and needs. I'm no longer living in a tent and wearing a uniform caked with desert sand, and I have no excuse for looking unkempt.

So I quickly finish up my shower and hop out to dry off and start hastily blow-drying my hair, which falls nearly to my mid-back by now. I glance over at the alarm clock perched on the nightstand and my heart skips a beat. I've wasted so much time already in the shower; it won't be much longer until Adrian gets here! I hurriedly shake most of the moisture out of my hair and start attempting to apply some minimal makeup, just enough to make me look more like a civilian. Because that's what I am nowadays.

But my hands shake as I try to put on eyeliner and mascara, and when I try to carefully dab some peachy-pink color onto my lips, I just feel silly. How do I prepare to meet the man who changed my life? It's been so long, and I don't even know who he is anymore. I have changed immeasurably since our night together in Afghanistan, so who is to say that he hasn't changed, too?

A horrible thought occurs to me: what if he is angry?

What if… what if he *knows?*

There is a secret to my transformation that I have kept from him. The one man who deserves to know more than anyone else. What if he has somehow figured it out? But I've been careful, kept a low profile. I've been more or less a recluse since I left military life and came back to rural Ontario to live with my aging parents in farm country.

What if he doesn't see me the same way? How did he even see me back then?

What if we don't connect the way we did before?

Suddenly, I am jolted from these paralyzing thoughts by a knock at the door. I freeze up, my eyes going wide as I glance over toward the doorway. I realize that I'm still naked, having gotten used to being alone in the privacy of my hotel room. I gulp and quickly pull the silk robe down from the hook by the bathroom door and wrap it around myself. I felt like a fool for taking so long to get ready. Adrian always was a fast traveler, a savvy driver who seemed to instinctively know the shortest, quickest routes to get absolutely anywhere.

And now he's here.

He knocks again and I rush to the door, taking a deep breath as I unhitch the deadlock and slowly pull the door open. My eyes travel up his hulking 6'3" frame, raking in his wide, powerful chest and thick arms, his muscles tight under the gray button-up shirt he's wearing with the sleeves rolled to his elbows. I have to tilt my head back slightly to look up at his glorious, gorgeous face.

Adrian is exactly as handsome as I remember. No, if anything he is more handsome now.

His once-cropped military crew cut has grown out somewhat, so that his dark blond hair sticks out in tousled tufts, and his usually-smooth jawline is peppered with a light shadow of stubble. He looks slightly older, more dignified. But there, in his jade-green eyes is a weighty sadness that wasn't there before. Like those eyes have seen horrors the likes of which I could never fathom. As though he has been traveling for far too long without rest or respite, only to end up standing on my doorstep, just waiting to walk back into my quiet life.

"Becca," he says, and a flicker of a fond smile plays upon his lips momentarily, and then disappears. He reaches out to cup the side of my face, and I can feel the scars and callouses of a hard life rough against my cheek. I find myself leaning into his touch hungrily. I have been waiting for this, even if I didn't acknowledge the fact until right this instant.

"Adrian, it's been so long," I murmur, turning to press a gentle kiss into the palm of his hand.

His lips fall open and he takes a half-step closer,

the gap between us smaller than before. It's easier to bridge with a swift, world-changing movement.

And without even another word, I rush into his arms and he lifts me up, my naked legs wrapping around his waist as he pushes into the room and peels the silky robe from around my shoulders to let it fall to the carpet. Our lips collide with a hard, heady passion as he rakes his fingers back through my still-damp hair, his tongue pushing into my mouth. He tastes so familiar, like commissary-grade peppermint toothpaste. Like gunpowder and desperation.

He leans me back onto the bed, standing up straight for a brief moment to unbutton his shirt and cast it aside before bending over and kissing me deeply. His rough, huge hands rove down my neck, my shoulders, caressing my breasts and brushing his thumbs over my erect nipples so that I let out a long, startled moan. Nobody has touched me this way… not since Adrian did, himself, two years ago.

He peels me open like a budding flower too early to fully bloom, unfolding my tightly-curled petals with insistent, yet gentle fingertips. Adrian sucks a trail of bruising, purple kisses down my neck and collarbone while his fingers slide between my thighs and stroke along my wet slit. I am so slick and ready for him, my body responding to his every touch with eager obedience, like I have been waiting for exactly this moment to set me free again.

"Oh, Bex," he groans, rutting against my bare thigh. It's a nickname nobody has called me in two years. He's the only one who calls me Bex. I tremble involuntarily at the triggered memory of the first time he mumbled the nickname this way, all breathless and needful under the desert moon.

I reach down to fondle the bulge at the front of his khaki pants, his enormous length stiff against my palm. "Please," I beg softly, "Adrian, I need you."

"I have dreamed of this moment," he replies in an undertone, unzipping his pants so that his massive cock springs free, bouncing in the open air. I spread my legs wide open for him, all former traces of guile or coyness gone instantaneously. There doesn't need to be any foreplay, any precession to our lovemaking. We don't need to lubricate the wheels of this machine to make it go. We simply fit together perfectly, like we are molded from the same lump of clay, two bodies folding into each other with graceful, unabashed desire.

I reach up to pull him down and kiss him with lightly biting teeth. He groans his appreciation and positions the head of his shaft at my slick opening, rubbing teasing circles around my aching cunt so that I whimper and dig my fingernails into his strong shoulders. I beg him with every breath and heave of my chest, I plead for him to spear me, to fill me up like he did before.

I have never needed anything so badly. So desperately.

"Please," I whisper, our eyes locking in that instant.

And without letting another moment pass, Adrian pushes his entire length into my pussy, spreading me open and splitting me in two with one smooth movement. I cry out and reach for him frantically, needing something to hold onto. He leans down to cradle me close to his chest, peppering my forehead with soft, reassuring kisses as he begins to thrust into me, striking that tight bud of delirious sensation inside me over and over again until I am spasming in his arms, my thighs shaking with every move.

"You feel so fucking good, Bex," Adrian murmurs, stroking my cheek, my hair. "I've been waiting for this, to hold you in my arms again, for so damn long."

"Am I dreaming?" I breathe, the words only barely audible.

He kisses me hard as he begins to lose control, fucking me more deeply with each thrust. It's nearly painful in its forcefulness, but I could not ask for less. This is exactly what I need. It's what I have craved for two long, lonely years. And by the sound of his pleasured groans, it seems that Adrian needs this just as badly as I do.

"You're not dreaming, babe," he assures me, fondling my breasts as he slams his enormous rod into my slippery cunt again and again until I'm crying out with the overwhelming crescendo of ecstasy, my body writhing under his expert machinations. He has me utterly under his command, and I could not deny him a single thing. He owns every inch of my body, every thread of my desire belongs to him, and him only. It always has, ever since we first looked across the crowded bazaar to find each other.

Finally, with a few final thrusts, Adrian bellows my name, "Oh god, Rebecca!" He shoots a hot spurt of his glorious seed deep within me, his cock twitching inside my pussy. He collapses beside me, covering my face in desperate kisses, stroking my cheeks. Adrian pulls me close to him while his honey slowly leaks out of me onto the expensive hotel bed sheets.

I am still tingling from the surreality of our reunion as his mouth finds my shoulder, kissing it tenderly. I am fully overwhelmed and overextended, and I know I need to sleep. But as the orgasm ebbs, there is a nagging, insistent thought digging in the back of my mind.

Things have changed. Irreparable, inevitable, irretrievable things.

I am not the same girl I was when we first met, even though my body responds to his in the same frenzied, needful way. He has changed, too; I can see it in his sad, beautiful eyes.

But I… well, I am a totally different woman now. My life is totally different now. Because I am a mother to a one-year-old daughter. And Adrian has no idea.

ADRIAN

There's so much that lights my fire about the girl in front of me. Even the way she looks as she thinks over the bombshell visit I dropped makes my heart pound, my shaft swelling every time I think about her.

My military service turned my body into a killing machine. Every reflex, every one of the muscles rippling down my body, my swollen arms, my very mind, all of it has been trained to react fast and strike hard. I'm a killer. I've done it all to protect what I love, but it's made me a deadly weapon.

Becca has been the one thing keeping my feet on the ground these past two years.

"I know this is unexpected," I say as I look down at her, gently taking her small hands in my large, tough ones. It feels so strange to be gentle with someone after all this time. "And I know it looks like

I want to move fast, but there's something about you, Becca," I say, looking into those gorgeous hazel eyes of hers and smiling.

It feels so fucking good to get this off my chest. I've heard of weaker men being anxious about sharing their feelings, wanting to keep everything pent-up until it dies. Not me. Life is too short and brutal for that. I need to tell this incredible woman everything she needs to hear about how I feel. Especially after our whirlwind lovemaking tonight, hours ago. It's midnight now and we are standing together in her upscale hotel room.

"I can't really explain it, but I feel a connection to you that goes deeper than the short time we had together."

She tilts her head to the side, even as her cheeks blush, and I give her hands a reassuring squeeze as I step forward. She doesn't step back, but tilts her neck up a little, an instinct that lets her expose herself to me almost unconsciously.

"I think I know what you mean," she says, her voice low and her eyes lidded as she looks up at me. It's unbelievable how validating it is for her to open herself up, but there's more to it than that.

"Not totally," I say. "Out in the field, doing everything I've been doing, the kind of violence I hope you're never exposed to... You get more in tune with feelings there are no words for, and there's something like that drawing me to you, Becca. I've had to do things no human should have to go through, all to protect our two countries. And all that gets blurry when you're putting your life on the line every day. Spending time away from what you're fighting for can make it all seem useless. But you? You've been in my mind the whole time, reminding me of it all."

Her eyes are shining, and her breath is getting quicker as I step closer, wrapping my arm around her waist and pulling her into me. I loom over her. She could bury her face in my chest standing on her tiptoes.

"I know it's a lot to take in, Becca," I say, my voice barely above a husky whisper as I let my hand run down her curves, my hands getting greedy as they grope her and take in a body that's even better than I remember it being. "But fuck it, if there's one thing I learned out on the killing fields, it's that life is too short to wait, and I'm done waiting. Every night, the thought of you kept me going, baby."

"Well?" she says, a smile playing across her round face as I press her into me. "How does the memory hold up in person?"

Words are weak. That much I've learned. Instead, I wrap my hand around the back of her neck, and I pull her into a deep, fierce kiss that warms her whole body.

The sound she makes, that disarmed gasp as my tongue delves into her lips and plays with her tongue, makes my heart pound harder, thumping against my chest as her blood runs hot in her cheeks.

"You drive me crazy every night," I growl into her ear, my scruff brushing against her cheek as I bring my lips to her ear, my hands gripping a bunch of that rich mahogany hair of hers. "We were only together *once*, and that was enough to keep me going for two years. I'm not going to lose you again, Becca. You're *mine*."

She gasps at that, a soft whimper full of desire that's been pent up for so, so long, and I feel a primal instinct within me to relieve it.

I have to restrain myself from ripping her shirt right off, and her bra falls away effortlessly, leaving her bare breasts exposed. I give myself just enough time to relish the sight of them, my eyes devouring her like a lion looks at its prey.

She practically melts in my grasp. I hold her up as if she weighs nothing, because to my hardened muscles, she really doesn't. Blood courses through my body and to my cock swiftly, and I'm ecstatic to see what this killer's body can do with the most intimate sides of life.

"I'm going to fuck you so hard you know every second of desire I went through for you, Becca," I say before pushing her down onto the bed and climbing onto it after her, looming over her small frame as she looks up at me with hunger in her eyes. It's the sweetest sight I could possibly imagine. This is the woman I fought for—fought both my enemies and myself.

I cup her breasts with my hands, squeezing and groping them, feeling every inch of sensitive flesh under me and feeling my cock grow in response. It's like the image of her has been imprinted on my mind like a lamb's silhouette is imprinted on a wolf's instincts. I feel something both baser and more distinct than lust for her as I bring my mouth down to her luscious tits.

My teeth graze her swollen, stiff nipples as I savor the taste of her dark areolas, and her gasps are like music to my ears as I torment them. My teeth graze and bite at one while my hand tends to the other, alternating between rubbing and flicking her nipple.

"I've wanted you so long, Adrian," she breathes, and I feel my cock stiffen and threaten to burst from my pants in sheer need. "I've gone so many nights wishing you were right here."

"I wanna give you your wish, baby," I growl, and without another word, I pull her pants down, along with her panties, bringing them down to her ankles and off her legs, tossing them aside.

My hands work her thighs first, strong fingers massaging her shapely legs as my eyes rove up and down them. She's so delicate. I forget how fragile civilians can seem compared to me, but Becca is like a porcelain doll in my grasp, and I feel like I could break her if I'm not careful.

In fact, I know I could.

But somehow, as I relish the sight of her naked body and the feel of her smooth legs, she looks up at me and senses what I'm thinking. Then she smiles, a simple, hungry smile that tells me she doesn't care. She's bold.

Bolder than some of the men I've killed.

I part her thighs and bring my face to her cunt, taking in the scent of her arousal and letting a deep, lustful groan from my chest that sends shivers up her body.

"My brothers in arms talked about missing the taste of food back home," I say, letting my hot breath wash over her pussy, "but me? This was the only thing I wanted on my tongue."

Before she can respond, I let out my tongue and draw it across her slit. She's so wet, so needy for me, and my massive, muscular body is ripe with lust to pour out and lavish all over her.

I send my tongue in deeper this time, really savoring the taste of her honey, and she cries out in a sudden ripple of feeling, her whole body awakening at my intimate touch. My tongue lashes out again and again, memorizing the feel and shape of her cunt. I moan blissfully into it, slipping a hand under the small of her back to hoist her up just a bit, making her an easier meal for me.

Her cunt is the ration I really wish I had while out there in the harsh Hindu Kush Mountains, hunting down and killing men I was ordered to. In comparison to the fantasies I had of taking her all over the world and lavishing her with trips she'd only dreamed of, this seems like a poor substitute, but it'll have to do for now.

Besides, I can't go another second without tasting her over and over again.

She tries desperately to push her hips up into my face, and I chuckle at her efforts. They feel so small and weak in my powerful grasp, but I help her along, my strong jaw holding her legs apart as much as they need to be.

My tongue emerges from her pussy to lavish the outer lips with attention, tasting every part of her. I could go in for the kill and drive her right to an orgasm, but I want to draw it out more.

I can practically feel the electricity in her body as she squirms around while the tip of my tongue traces back and forth across her lower lips, teasing her deliciously. She tries to resist it, pushing up needily into me, but I draw back, a smile tugging on my lips as I eat her out.

"Don't keep me waiting, Adrian," she begs me, and my hardened heart warms at her request, but I'm not going to give in that easily.

My tongue wanders slowly, deliberately up to the hood of her clit, where it swirls around the outside while I reach to her tits and start toying with them again.

"Oh god," she gasps, "Adrian, oh my god, please!"

I let out a low, dark purr as my tongue dips ever so slowly towards her clit, but then draws out just before touching it, and she squeals in need, wrapping her legs around my neck as my thumbs rub her nipples. *"Adrian...!"*

Finally, I let loose and dive into her lips. My tongue roves hungrily up her slit and right to her clit, which strikes with deadly precision, and immediately, she cries out as her abs tighten and relax, and I feel her honey flooding my mouth as I lap up her cunt again, then going to the same place, tormenting her swollen, needy, wet nub.

Her clit is my victim. My tongue lashes out and strikes it over and over again, and she starts to buck her hips up, but I hold her down, depriving her of any control of my torture. My tongue is going to have the satisfaction it's wanted for so long, and I'm going to keep her exposed and vulnerable to it.

Again and again, my tongue tastes her sweet honey and brings it up to her clit to wash it over and over with her own come. I could be here for hours, and at the thought that I'll be able to torture her whenever I want—from the time she wakes up in the morning to the time she goes to bed at night—I get more aggressive, taking more of her pussy into my mouth with every long lap.

My tongue delves deep into her cunt, and my teeth graze her clit, and she screams out again as she comes, legs squeezing tight around my head.

At long last, I raise my head, my impeccable body looming over her and looking at the damage I've done to this poor woman.

Her chest is already rising and falling visibly as she breathes, trying to keep a hold of herself as I ruin her. I feel pride swelling in my chest at the sight of my handiwork. And I haven't even taken my cock out yet.

I start to reach down and undo my pants, but finding some untapped strength in her, Becca sits up, crawling into her knees and reaches for my belt. She looks up at me with doe eyes, licking her lips and gazing at me as though asking permission. I grant it with a stroke of her hair and a loving look, and her fingers expertly undo the front of my pants and reach in for my cock.

My shaft is enormous, and every time she lets her fingers glide across it, her eyes drinking it all in, I feel another wave of desire crash through me. My cock picks up on it and stands stiffer than ever, its massive crown bulging and dark.

She leans forward and opens her mouth, those beautiful lips parting to take the head of my cock into her mouth while a hand drifts to my balls. She sighs into me as she feels their weight, their virility, their power.

The look on her face is one of pure bliss as she lets her tongue brush against the tip of my cock, and it sends heat up my shaft and through my torso, warming me to the bone. I let out a groan as she starts to have her fun, running her tongue around the edges of the crown, savoring the shape and sheer girth of what she's been deprived of for so long.

As she starts to work her mouth further down my shaft, I let my large fingers toy with locks of her hair, gently tugging at it as I roll my fingers through the sea of dark brown. "I don't know how I went two years without you, baby."

She moans in response, her eyes turning up to me again full of desire, full of repressed lust she's been keeping under the surface for so long. Lust I know I have, too.

Her mouth works further and further up my shaft, to the point that I'm surprised she can fit so much of it into her mouth. To my delight, I see a hint of pride in her face as it touches the back of her throat. Then she lets her tongue roll down the bottom of my cock.

I never realized how good she was at this. My whole body starts to unwind at the feeling of that powerful muscle pressing against my cock, caressing it ecstatically, hungrily.

I reward her efforts with a light tug of her hair, and the sensation makes her moan delightedly. Her tonguing gets steadier, and she grows bolder, moving her mouth around to get just the right angle as she covers my shaft with her tongue, letting the back of her tongue massage my crown with every movement.

This is my girl.

I start to feel my cock tensing, readying itself to go over the point of no return, and Becca knows it. She grows more enthusiastic, desperately trying to get that sweet seed out of me as she works harder, whimpering and sighing with every lick of my monstrous cock.

Just before I tip over the brink, I take a tighter hold of Becca's hair, pulling her back gently while she looks up at me in profound protest.

She gives a whimper, a pouting lip stuck out as I tug her back onto the bed, but my cock is glistening and more swollen with need than ever. I'm not about to let her get off so easily.

She sits on her legs, looking at me like I've just taken something precious from her. To dispel the sorrow in her eyes, I seize her and kiss her lips, tasting myself on them and plunging my tongue into her, letting her taste herself on my mouth. She gasps at the gesture, and I see those irresistible cheeks blushing lightly when I pull away.

But there's no sweetness in my tone when I hold her chin up and lean in to growl into her ear: "On your knees."

Immediately, obediently, Becca gets on all fours

on the bed, looking up at me in anticipation, and I pull that cute ass of hers around to face me.

I give it a sharp slap, making her yelp and push it further up, desperate for me.

"I want to feel you again, Adrian," she gasps, clutching fistfuls of the bedsheets in front of her as she looks back at me, eyes shining at my looming, massive cock. "I've needed you so long, Adrian!"

I reach out and grab her hair, pulling it back enough to make her back arch, a gasp of pleasure. With my other hand, I stroke her ass in admiration, feeling the soft flesh and grasping it.

"Do you have any idea how much I missed this ass?" I growl, and before she can answer, I plunge my cock into her waiting, soaking cunt.

Immediately, she lets out a long, bliss-filled sigh when my head slides up her inner walls. I remember exactly where her g-spot is, angling myself to thrust my cock right up against that most sensitive point in her body.

I waste no time in pounding into her, holding onto her hair like a leash while my hand holds her hips, angling her just the way I want.

She's so easy to physically manipulate in my powerful hands, and I make sure she knows it. When she starts to slip, I hold her up and tug back on her hair, and I feel her abs tightening as she draws closer and closer to orgasm.

Her breasts are swaying under her as my long,

hard cock pummels her g-spot, grinding against it with each piston-like thrust I deliver to her, and I'm insatiably rhythmic. I want to take in every inch of her pussy, reveling in the way she feels, the way she tightens when I pound into her just so.

My balls have been swinging heavily under me, but at last, I feel them start to tighten, and my cock swells larger than ever as I let out a long groan and feel precum beading up at my cock, pulsing and twitching within.

"I'm gonna come inside you, Becca," I groan, "I want the world to know you're *mine.*"

With that, she lets out a ragged moan, her sigh punctuated by the sensation of warmth rippling up her body as the orgasm hits her, and I start pounding harder and harder, letting myself topple over the edge with abandon.

I've waited for this kind of freedom, fought hard for it, and I'm holding nothing back as I take her hips with both hands and hold on as I start to lose my rhythm. The fierce fucking loses its machine-like regularity and staggers into bestial passion.

My balls tense, and I let my mouth hang open before I let out a sharp, deep groan, and hot seed shoots out of my shaft, pulsing in sweet release along with her orgasm. Her honey is flooding my pulsing cock, which feels so red-hot that I'm worried about hurting her as my powerful pulses pour more and more of my seed into her.

"Ohhhh, ohh fuck, Adrian!" she cries out, utterly uninhibited as I empty myself into her aching pussy. There's even more of it now than there was before, and I swell with pride at the thought that my cock is growing even more potent inside her, if that were possible.

Finally, my pulsing come subsides, and I slowly pull my glistening shaft from her as we flop down onto the bed next to each other, breathing heavily in the afterglow.

I take Becca's hand in mine and raise it to my mouth, kissing it gently before she spoons into me and my strong arms wrap around her. I kiss her neck while I massage her overstimulated cunt, and she whimpers in delight, scooting closer to me before giving a contented sigh.

"I've never been in any *real* danger all this time," she whispers, her voice the sweetest sound I've ever heard. "But I still never feel safer than when I'm in your arms, Adrian."

I let out a soft murmur in response, the scent of her hair in my face as I breathe slowly for a long time before I speak.

"I've had this plan in my head to sink a chunk of the money I've been saving up," I say, my voice still thick with lust. "I've got enough to put us anywhere we want for life, but I've been thinking about home."

"Home?" she asks, curiosity in her voice as she

turns her head back, then turns around to face me, propping herself up on an elbow, smiling, glowing.

"Yeah," I say with a smile. "I'm a country boy, after all, and that never really leaves you. I want to build a place out in Ontario, somewhere rural. Out of the way. Somewhere quiet."

She bites her lip as she smiles, eyes shining as she watches me. "Log cabin out in the woods, built with your own two hands?"

"Somethin' like that," I chuckle. "But I'm thinking more of a farm, somewhere where I can start providing for you by *making* life rather than taking it. A nice, sturdy barn with everything we'd need, plenty of good pasture land… and a big ranch-style house, just for us, where we can start our family.

Something changes in her, and the smile fades from my face for a moment. Have I said too much? Gone too far? But no, it isn't that, there's something else written in those beautiful features, something I can't quite place.

"Well," she says, and this time, it's her who looks hesitant, reluctant, and I watch her intently, furrowing my eyebrows. "That sounds like something out of a dream come true."

"Then what's the matter, baby?" I ask, taking her chin in my fingers and looking at her with concern. "You can't pretend something's not bothering you."

"I don't mean it like that," she says hurriedly, sitting up in bed, worrying her lip a moment before continuing. "I want this, Adrian. I want this for us. You're right—life is too short to hesitate, I want to jump in and build a life with you!"

I smile, but I look at her as though egging her on to continue, and she lowers her eyes a moment before wringing some of the sheets in her hands.

"It's just that I've kinda... gotten a head start on building a family."

I blink at her in utter confusion, and finally, she looks me in the eye.

"Adrian... I had a baby while you were away. I-I'm a mother now."

I watch him nervously, just waiting for his handsome face to twist into a rageful frown. I wait for him to scream at me, to shove me away like I'm damaged goods like most guys would. Without my daughter around, it's almost like I can pass myself off the way I used to: a confident, sexually available single woman. This whole entire week that I've been staying alone in Mississauga without my baby, men have watched me closely with their hungry eyes, drinking in my aloneness, my vulnerability. After Maya was born, I had to shed my former ability to turn heads. Men simply didn't want to notice me anymore, overlooking me because I was disqualified for having too much baggage in the form of a stroller and diaper bag.

Suddenly, I was no longer a potential mate, no longer desirable to male eyes. I was just a mother, a faceless blob of maternal instinct upon which no man could hang his lusty dreams.

But being alone here in this city reminded me of what it was like before Maya came into my life. I was seen as a romantic object once again, only this time, I noticed the difference. I don't want to be an object anymore. I want to be a fully independent person, not defined solely by either my sexual availability or my status as a good mother.

And as soon as Adrian came waltzing back into my world, there would have to be a change, eventually. He still looked at me as though I were just the same single woman he met overseas, accessible and available. Ripe for the picking. If he were any other man, I might have kept my baby a secret from him. If he had only wanted to come into my life for this one night in some nostalgic attempt to relive the fiery but quickly extinguished passion of our first time together in the desert, then I could have just withheld the truth without feeling too badly. After all, I would never want to drag him into fatherhood kicking and screaming, nor do I want him to stick around just out of some bland obligation. I don't want some loveless partnership, or a tedious obligation to arrange meetings for my kid. I want a real love, starting with me.

But Adrian… talking about moving to the country, building our own home, working the land… and starting a family. Well, I never expected that. I assumed he was only here for the moment, just to quickly blow in and out of my life in a blur like he did before. I assumed I was just a pit stop, a little dalliance on the side before he was catapulted away from me and back into the jaws of imminent danger, just like he did when his mission took him out of my life.

I figured he would ignite a fire in my soul and then leave me burning out alone again.

And in some ways, it might have been easier if he had. I could simply collect the scattered shreds of my dignity and move on, holding the memory of a second one-night stand in the back of my mind for ages, to warm me in my coldest moments. But now… well, things are different.

I just know that in this moment, he is seeing me differently. Through a new lens.

And I am terrified to hear what he has to say. Terrified of his reaction. I expect anger, disappointment, disgust, betrayal. I expect to see his interest in me fade away to nothing instantaneously now that there is an obstacle to our smooth sailing in the form of my precious, lovely daughter. His green eyes flash with unnamable emotions and I start to look away, wincing as I prepare for him to make a thousand excuses to leave, to escape before I can sink my man-trapping claws into him and force him to be a father. At least, I assume that's what he must think of me.

But instead, he reaches forward to cup my cheek

and turn my face back toward him. There is a faint smile on his lips and he shakes his head. I await his words anxiously, holding my breath.

"Bex, I never knew," he says softly. "How—how old is the baby?"

My stomach lurches. Surely he will put two and two together, but I'm not ready to explore that issue yet. I'm not prepared to talk about it. Not now. Not here. Still, he is waiting for me to respond and I can't leave him hanging.

"She's about a year old," I answer quietly, hoping he doesn't probe too much further.

"She?" Adrian repeats, his smile widening as his eyebrows lift up slightly. He looks… well, he looks downright pleased. I'm surprised at this development, having expected him to freak out.

"Yeah. Her name is Maya," I tell him, and a smile plays at my own lips at the mere mention of my baby girl. Even in a tense moment like this, I can't help but feel a rush of maternal adoration for my child. I am proud of her. I love her fiercely. Even if her existence complicates every element of my life, she is more than worth the complication.

"Maya," Adrian says reverently, and as his lips form her name I feel my heart skip a beat.

A part of me – a very large part of me – hopes I can manage to hold onto her and Adrian at the same time. I realize with a surge of uncomfortable warmth that I don't want to lose him. Whether I acknowledged it consciously or not, a small but dogged part of me has been wishing for some way to find him again, longing for him to come back into my life. And now, here he is. And he knows the truth!

Well, at least he knows *part* of the truth.

Maybe I should confess now, before this goes any further. It's only the right thing to do, I tell myself, gritting my teeth as I prepare to tell him everything. But before I can open my mouth to say another word, Adrian leans forward and kisses me sweetly.

Peering deeply into my eyes, he says, "Rebecca Summers, I don't care who the baby's father is. I don't care what has happened in the two years I've been away. I never forgot about you, even for a moment. You have been in my heart all this time, and I think I know why now."

I hold my breath, my lungs tightening up as I await his next words. Does he know?

But he grins and says, "It's fate, Bex. You and I… we're meant to be. I know that to be the truth. I can feel it. And I know you feel it, too."

I am dumbfounded, just staring at him blankly. This is certainly not how I pictured this confrontation to proceed, but I am overwhelmed with joy at the knowledge that he feels just as drawn to me as I am to him. He feels the same magnetic attraction that I do.

We want each other.

No, we *need* each other.

Regardless of circumstance. Regardless of the future.

"I do," I reply, nodding. "I feel the same way, Adrian. I just... I was so afraid to tell you. I didn't want you to see me differently. To treat me differently. My life has changed a lot in two years, but the way I feel about you... well, that has remained totally the same. I've thought about you so many times, wondering where you are and what you're doing. Praying that you were doing okay. I don't know why, but I just couldn't get you out of my mind, no matter what happened."

That is only partly a lie. In addition to my overwhelming feelings of attraction and fondness for Adrian, there is also another huge reason as to why he was always in my thoughts. But I can't tell him about that just yet. It's just too soon.

I need time to figure things out, to feel this out. I want to be sure before I drop that bombshell. I can't play fast and loose with something as precious and precarious as my daughter's life. I need to know, first and foremost, if this thing — whatever it is — that I have with Adrian is for real. I need to know that he is going to stick around, and not just because Maya is his. I want him to be in my life for no other reason than love. I need stability, and so does Maya.

"I have seen so many horrible things. Hell, I have done some of those horrible things, myself. But the thought of you has sustained me through all of it, Bex. You have been my bright light in the darkest hours of my life these past years. I don't know what it is. I can't quite put my finger on it, but somewhere in my soul I knew all along. It's you. It's always been you," Adrian tells me fervently, pulling me close to him. I rest my head on his hard, muscular chest and close my eyes.

"And your baby… Maya. If she is your flesh and blood then I will love her as my own. I already feel like I love her in my heart, even though we've never met," he says, pushing me back gently to gaze warmly into my face. It's incredible how sweet, how gentle he can be, when I know that these same hands that hold me so tenderly have wrung the life out of others.

"I love every part of you, Rebecca. And your daughter is part of you."

My stomach twists into knots at the word love. I know he means it in a less pointed fashion, that I should keep my head on straight and not let my love-soaked daydreams get the best of me. There is still a massive divide between us. An enormous lie, a sin of omission, digging out a canyon between the two of us, even still.

For a moment, I toy with the idea of just telling him. Bursting out with the heavy truth that's weighing down my tongue. I could do it. So easily. I could just say the words that would alter our relationship forever. It could push him away from me, or it could draw us closer together. Either way, it would be a mighty shock, and we are just so new together. He's only just gotten back from god knows what kinds of dark places and deeds, and it isn't the right time.

Besides, I have to be careful for Maya's sake. If this works out, then great. No, better than great. But if something happens, if we don't work together like we want to, like we plan to… then I don't want the messy complications of fighting for custody. I don't want to lose Adrian and Maya in one poorly calculated fell swoop. Being a mother means being cautious. It means putting my daughter's needs before mine. But I can't help but feel a little selfish — I want to keep her for myself.

I need to know first of all that Maya and Adrian will get along. It is difficult to imagine this powerful, deadly hulk of a man cradling and caring for such a tiny, fragile soul. What if he can't totally put his past behind him? What if he is hiding some trauma that will sneak out and jeopardize us all when we least expect it? I don't know where he's been all this time. For all I know, his past could still be haunting his every footstep. And I'll be damned if I allow something so shadowy and insidious to haunt my young daughter's life, as well.

And if I tell him now— the whole truth— what if he is angry with me? Hell, of course he will be angry with me. Adrian will feel betrayed. Cheated. He could act in revenge, try to take my baby away from me as punishment for hiding the reality of her parentage.

No. It's not time yet. I have to wait until I have more information, until I'm sure. I'll take him home. Introduce him to my parents, and Maya. I'll see how he reacts.

Then I'll tell him that Maya is his child, too. That he is the father.

I've heard a lot about people having a hard time adjusting to civilian life again. The transition is so hard for so many that it destroys lives. I'm lucky enough to have Becca at my side, though, and with her, I feel like I can do anything. Go anywhere. And that's just what I'm gonna do.

I watch as the highway passes us by, Mississauga shrinking in the rear view mirror as we make our way into Toronto. She's just finished her latest contract, and I want to treat her to a romantic mini-vacation before we head out to her parent's house. It's late, but I booked the swankiest place I could find on short notice, and though the area seems a little rough, the hotel is beautiful. I quickly check us in, my eyes roaming the white and gold lobby with appreciation. It really does deserve its name. *The Grand.*

By the time our elevator door opens on the top floor, I'm carrying Becca in my arms on the way to our room, and once inside, I tuck her into bed carefully, planting a kiss on her head as she snuggles into the sheets with a smile on her face, her eyes cracking open just enough to glance up at me lovingly.

"Night..." she says groggily before turning over, and I take a quick shower before slipping into bed with her. The military trains you to be able to fall asleep fast, so it's only a few seconds before I drift off into a deep sleep.

※

I fire my weapon at the face that appears around the corner holding a woman at gunpoint. In a flash, he crumples to the ground before the rest of my team can even turn their barrels on him, and the Kurdish woman dashes away with a terrified scream, back outside the now-vacant complex that made up an IS compound.

"Clear," says my second-in-command.

All of us hold strategic positions in the now-ruined command room. We wear black, masks over our faces that make us as invisible as our activities will be on all official reports. This Syrian night will leave no trace of our presence but the memory of what we've done in the minds of the local village's people.

I strip my mask off and stride over to the table full of documents the enemy had out upon our arrival. The leader's blood stains some of them, and I push his lifeless body from its chair so I can get a better look at the information.

We've been stalking this cell for weeks. Each operation requires more patience and stealth than any ordinary soldiers are trained to handle. We're Navy SEALs. We do not exist, yet we're everywhere, and when we strike, success is absolute.

Each of the men around me has been put through the most rigorous training the United States can offer. We're towering specimens of our species, rippling with muscle that's poised to react to anything at a moment's notice, and every eye is scanning the room for unnoticed activity.

We are prepared for everything, because with missions as deadly as ours, anything can go wrong.

"It's all here," I say softly, glancing through the documents written in Arabic. "We were right. They've been moving supplies in through the northwest, hoping to take the city. But this was the serpent's head. Good work, men."

The rest of my squad gives the faintest of nods in acknowledgement, except for my lieutenant. He has his hand at his earpiece, and I can read his concern in his eyes.

"What's the matter?" I ask. His eyes narrow, and he looks up at me with sudden alarm.

"Sir! Intel just reported in. They miscalculated. Russian special forces has this location on their radar, they're going after the same target we just eliminated."

"What?!" I snap, muscles tensing, my mind racing with the various strategies the Russians are prone to using for operations like this. "Notify our contact immediately, make sure they know w-"

My words are cut off as a flashbang grenade goes off behind us, and I'm blinded as my body's reflexes force me to return to one of the cover spots I memorized on the way in here. Damn rookie mistake, and we're out of time: the Russians are here, and they think *we're* the enemy.

Bullets start flying the next moment, and I hear the sound of a body hitting the ground where my communications officer was standing a few moments ago.

I force my eyes to regain function, and I hear shouting in Russian as the shadow operatives spill into the room. The Spetsnaz are the Russian Special Forces. They're quick, efficient, and trained under utterly brutal conditions. If either side wants to survive this, we all need to act quickly.

Our training kicks in, and we begin responding as a single unit. My squad mate nearest to me provides covering fire at the doorway where the shouting is coming from, and as soon as his assault rifle goes off, I move across the room, keeping low and in cover.

In the briefest of moments, I glimpse the Spetsnaz operatives firing at us. They wear ski masks not unlike ours, but I can identify their leader. He's positioned at the most advantageous spot to dole out verbal and nonverbal commands, and his men operate like clockwork around him.

One of them is headed straight for my destination. He points his gun at me, but I'm faster, firing off a single round that puts him down.

"On your six!" one of my men shouts, and I whirl around at catch the wrist of the man driving a knife down towards me. The blood on his blade tells me he's killed another one of my men. This operation is going south very quickly, and we need to move.

I clench my hand and shatter the wrist of my attacker, delivering a hard strike to his stomach. There's no room for theatrics here. There's a team full of killers who know this man intimately, and in about two seconds, their bullets are going to be filling my torso.

So I wrench the knife from the man's broken hand and drive it into his eye, deep into the skull. The next moment, I'm low to the ground as bullets whiz by where I was a moment ago.

I hear the telltale metal clinking of a grenade landing to my right, just beside where one of my men is engaged in hand-to-hand combat with one of the Russians. I lunge for it, seizing the live grenade and hurling it out the doorway, where I see the leader shout at his men before they dive for cover. The grenade goes off with a bang that leaves all our ears ringing.

In the chaos, I stand up and plunge my dagger into the back of the skull of the man my squad mate is engaged with. I grab him and pull him to cover as the enemy leader reappears, his assault rifle raised and fury in his eyes.

I know what happens in situations like this. The leader's ego is getting to him. He's not going to be willing to back down in a situation like this. The idiot's going to get more men killed on both sides than is necessary. I've got to make a decision, and I've got to make it quick.

Even as my men trade fire, I know the doorway is just a choke point we'd be filing into. There's a single window in the room, but it's exposed, and my men need cover. My hand goes to my vest as I crouch, and over our comms, I give the order to initiate a protocol my men know by heart.

By the time I'm pulling the pin out of the smoke grenade, my men are already disengaging from the enemy and retreating to the window. I lob the thing into the midst of the Russians, and before most of them can flip their goggles over their eyes, it goes off with a bang, and thick, dark smoke fills the room.

I'm going to be the last one out. No way in hell

am I letting any of my men leave after me. One after the other, I confirm my men's exit, but as I expected, not all of the Russians are blinded by the grenade.

A silhouette appears in the smoke, and I recognize the leader of the Russians immediately. I drop the knife of the man I killed, letting it clatter to the ground. My hand is poised to draw my own blade, but I want to give this bastard the chance to walk away from this unharmed.

I see his features more clearly as he steps closer. His face mask has been blown off by the grenade I threw back at him, and he's bleeding from several shrapnel wounds. One of his eyes is clenched tight, and I can see blood running through the eyelid. I've just cost him an eye along with two of his squad mates. He's a hardened older man with graying hair and a square jaw. I know this isn't going to end peacefully. But I don't want them to think we didn't give them to chance to keep their lives.

"We aren't enemies," I say in Russian, keeping my tone even, but without a word, he lunges for me, his hand held tight like a spear aimed at my throat. I parry the maneuver and sweep his legs out from under him, but he recovers flawlessly, drawing his knife and swiping at my Achilles tendon with the blade. I roll away with the strike, but I feel the knife graze the thick leather of my boot. I was milliseconds from death. This guy is good.

"You made an enemy," he growls as I draw my

knife and meet his next attack. I catch his wrist, but this one won't be so easily broken. Unfortunately for him, he finds the same unexpected toughness in me.

I bring my knee up and strike him in the diaphragm, and he takes the blow with a grunt. As I twist around to get a grip on his arm and end this fight before the smoke clears, I realize his other hand has gone for his pistol, and he brings it up towards my head.

Looking down the barrel of a gun is an experience you don't forget. Time around you slows, and all you can focus on is that unfeeling cylinder of metal that might well be your ticket into the next word the next instant.

But my body isn't like that of other men. Like a supernatural force, my reflexes spin me around, hurling the Russian over my back as the gun goes off right next to my head, and I'm utterly deafened by the sound.

I don't stop to follow up on the move. My men are down the rope, and I propel myself out, grabbing onto the rope and racing to the ground.

Moments later, my men and I are rappelling down the building out the window, into the cool air of the Syrian night. Even as we do, we haven't let down our guard. This isn't a retreat. It's a shift in battlefields.

As we expected, there are more of the Russians outside, and we find ourselves under fire the moment we're out into the air. We return it, but even as we make our descent, one of my men takes a bullet to the chest, and the gurgling grunt that comes from him tells me he's a dead man in hours if I don't get him to medical attention soon.

Bullets are raining down on us as we reassume positions in the rocky outcroppings that once provided the natural defenses for this compound.

I have four men remaining out of my five, and I'm not about to lose any more.

"Hold this position," I order my men before getting on the line with Intel. "We need an extraction, we're coming out hot!" I can hardly hear anything out of my right ear.

The sounds of the bullets firing all around us are loud yet somehow muffled, dull pops, each one piercing the air with such deadly fury that I feel my heart pounding faster and faster, each boom shattering the air around me.

Our backup isn't going to come. Another grenade hits the ground, and my men take cover. The blast sends shrapnel and sharp rocks flying everywhere.

Images flash before my eyes at a thousand miles a minute. I see the gun barrel pointed at my eyes again just as I hear the gunshot. I see bullets riddling my squad mate, his body hitting the ground as more ring out all around us. I see my own bullet hurdling into the Russian I killed, a man who wasn't even supposed to be here. The faces of each of the IS insurgents flash by, the Kurdish woman, my men, the Russian leader. The barrel of the gun again, hammer hitting the back of the bullet as it rockets toward my face.

Another boom.

❧

Becca's voice is calling out to me as I wake up. I'm on my feet, heart pounding its way out of my chest as I hold onto the open window with both hands, knuckles white, eyes staring at the world outside as fireworks explode high in the air above and down on the street.

My pupils are dilated, and every muscle in my body is tense. My grip is cutting into the wood windowsill, and I'm just staring out into the world outside. I become vaguely aware of the cool air. I'm shirtless. Where are my fatigues? Where are my weapons? Why is Becca here?

"Adrian! Adrian, come away from the window!" Her voice is muffled like the booming sounds outside. I blink, covering my face, and as she takes a step forward towards me, I whip around, glaring at her.

There's hardly any recognition in my eyes, and I have to fight my instincts tooth and nail to keep from attacking her. Like waking from a half-dreaming state, I'm still trying to figure out why I don't hear shouts in Russian around me, my killing instinct fueling adrenaline that pumps through my bloodstream.

"Adrian, you're—there's no danger!" she says, her voice clear and loud yet somehow gentle. Becca. It's Becca. My Bex.

My heart is still racing, and I blink hard at her, and I start to hear her clearly when another firework goes off outside behind me, and I move back to the bed, searching for... for something, I don't know what. Maybe my gun, a knife, something.

I feel a hand laid on my shoulder, and without a second thought, I whip around and seize it by the wrist, glaring into the terrified eyes of its owner, her eyes just as wide as mine in the glint of the midnight streetlights outside.

I walk toward Adrian slowly with both my arms raised, my eyes wide and my heart hammering away in my chest as I stare down this heaving, riled-up beast of a man. I feel like I'm walking into a lair of wolves, approaching the pack leader to remove a thorn from his mighty paw. I can hear my own blood rushing rhythmically in my ears as I step closer to him. His calloused fingers are still wrapped around my fragile wrist, and I know it would only take a second's movement for him to crush my delicate bones in his fist. He is a massive beast of strength and power, but there is a sheen of something akin to primal fear lurking behind his wild eyes.

"Adrian, Adrian, it's me," I murmur softly, gazing up into his face. His eyes start to soften slightly, but he doesn't let go of my wrist yet. There's a long silence, and just when I think he is about to let go and calm down, another round of bright red fireworks crackle and explode in the sky beyond our hotel room window. He lets out a bellow and pulls me close, shielding me with his huge, muscular frame as though to protect me from flying shrapnel or enemy fire.

"Watch out!" he exclaims as several more white rockets burst in the sky, the deafening crack causing him to push me to the floor and kneel down, still trying to physically protect me from some unseen, imaginary attack. I know what this is. I have seen it many times during my work as a NATO official. This is post-traumatic-stress disorder, and I know that while I am aware that the fireworks pose no threat to our well-being, Adrian has been thrust painfully back into the throes of war. In this moment, he cannot tell the difference between the explosion of a celebratory firework for Canada Day and the sickening crack of enemy fire.

"Adrian! Listen, come back to me!" I shout over the din of fireworks. He is crouched over me, his chest pressing against the side of my head. I can hear and feel his rampaging heartbeat. For all he knows, we are back in the desert, with gunshots and bombs going off left and right. Adrian thinks we are in imminent danger. And his first instinct is to shield me from it. To rescue me.

"Get down and stay down!" he orders, wrapping

his arms around me tightly. I am suddenly transported backward, too, but not to the heat of battle.

I am propelled into the past, to when I first saw Adrian across the busy marketplace and our eyes locked, cementing that moment in my thoughts forever. Then I remember hearing his vehicle rolling down the dunes to the camp, where I waited for him one day to drop off a manila folder of classified information my NATO team had uncovered. Tactical information that would aid the SEALs in a mission I knew very, very little about. I had been waiting for over an hour, and getting very impatient, standing there in the blistering hot desert sunshine.

I remember seeing that desert-worn vehicle rumbling toward the camp, toward his tent where I was waiting for him. That vehicle had scratch marks all over it, barely a drop of paint left, and roared like a beast. But one thing it did have going for it was an old-timey radio and cassette player. And that day, Adrian was blasting a bootleg Joseph Castello cassette he had dug out of a pile of mostly-stolen goods at the bazaar a week prior.

As he pulled up and turned off the car, I heard the closing bassline of *Walking Through Fire*. I can distinctly recall the flutter in my chest as Adrian hopped out of the car, whipped off his dark shades, and sauntered over to me with a broad, charismatic grin. He was a showstopper, even then, even covered in desert dust and grime, smelling of diesel fuel and commissary aftershave.

He had opened his mouth and said cockily, "Are you real or a mirage?"

Of course, I rolled my eyes at the time. But now, I would kill to get him back to that state of mind. I would do anything to bring Adrian back to the present moment, to make him feel real and safe again. To see that cocksure attitude straighten his shoulders and clear his foggy gaze.

So I do the only thing I can think to do. It makes no sense, but it's my first instinct. And my years with NATO taught me many things, not least of which was not to question my instincts. Sometimes, when you're in a crisis, the best thing you can do is the first thing you think of.

I start to sing, softly.

"*When times are hard, and there's nowhere else to turn,*" I sing, hoping desperately that this will be the trick to bringing Adrian back out of his PTSD episode. It's silly. It's absurd. But right now, it's all I can think to do.

"*I keep looking through the licking flames and know it's bound to burn,*" I continue, singing louder, even though I can't possibly reach the low notes like the singer could and I don't try. "*But I know you're mine, waiting on the other side.*"

Even though the fireworks continue to blast outside, illuminating the night sky with streaks of red and white, as I sing the next verse I can feel Adrian starting to freeze up, his muscles tensing and going still as he listens to me. I hope to goodness this is working, because I feel like more than a little bit of an idiot for doing this. I never sing except for in the shower, or occasionally to Maya. But if it works, then it's worth all the potential embarrassment.

"And even though the fire marks my flesh, I know you're mine, waiting on the other side."

Adrian starts to loosen up, and I slowly, carefully turn around to sit in front of him as he kneels on one knee, almost like the position a man would take when proposing marriage. Every time a firework bursts in the sky, I can see him wince, physically shaken by the triggering sound. But now that animalistic rawness is gone from his eyes. He isn't in fight or flight mode anymore. He looks softer, more like he's still in the present moment. I watch as his distant gaze comes back into focus, his beautiful green eyes still trained on my own face while I sing.

Like I am his grounding point. His tether to the current reality.

"And even as the night grows dark, and I feel like I'm done in, I think of you and your face," I go on, reaching out to gently touch his tightening, stubble-rough jaw with one trembling hand. It feels bizarrely as though I am trying to befriend a wild animal, ready for the inevitable bite at any moment. But it doesn't come. Instead, Adrian seems to almost melt into my touch,

his eyes closing as he leans toward my hand. I caress his cheek fondly, stroking the sharp, chiseled cut of his jaw. I hold my breath anxiously as I encircle him with my arms, though he is too broad-chested for me to wrap them all the way around his muscular torso. I pull him to me and guide him to lie down with his head in my lap.

"It's okay, I'm here," I tell him quietly, stroking his hair and marveling at the massive, heavily-muscled, cold-blooded killer of a man resting peacefully in my lap. Adrian is powerful. He is a mass of relentlessly-trained instincts and carefully-honed physical perfection. Hell, when I first met him, I was almost afraid of him, even though by that point I was certainly used to spending time around other militant, buff, crude-mannered men.

In the camp in Afghanistan, I was constantly surrounded by guys in fatigues, in dust-covered, fuel-smeared, tight-fitting white shirts. Their muscles bulged almost as much as their egos did, and I watched my fair share of tough guys fight each other over the stupidest things. They were well-trained, of course, to deal with combat and stress. But at that moment, it felt like we were all living in the eye of the storm, just waiting for the next shoe to drop. So all the men were restless and antsy, hating the fact they had to sit tight and wait in such a dreary place. They craved action — of all kinds.

But the camp was rather like a pit stop, almost

like a purgatory or state of limbo for those who had just emerged from battle and those who were poised on the verge of another round of combat service. I was there to look out for the welfare of both soldiers and local Afghans, making sure everyone had enough rations, clothing, drinking water, and toiletry goods to get by with relative comfort. As much comfort as one could manage in the middle of a dusty, war-rattled desert, anyway. Which is to say, not very much.

I was making the rounds one day, walking through the crowded bazaar to talk to some of my favorite vendors and check in with them. It was a very windy day, and I had to wear a visor and veil to help keep the sand out of my eyes. But I went to my favorite fabrics vendor, an older woman named Saba, to ask her how her family was doing. Her daughter had recently given birth to the family's first grandson, and they were all over the moon about it, even with the climate of strife and destruction hanging heavily in the air. As a NATO liaison, it was part of my job to keep tabs on the local community and look out for their needs and concerns. It was my favorite part of the job, one that I took very seri-ously, even though most of my team members rolled their eyes at me for it. Many of my coworkers viewed the native population as part of the faceless mass they thought of as "the enemy," but I knew that to be incorrect and wildly unfair to the genuine human beings who happened to live in the area. So I went above and beyond to make connections, to learn about the local culture, to help maintain a working relationship.

As I pulled down my veil to greet Saba in my very broken Pashto, she grinned up at me, digging in her pocket to fish out a Polaroid photograph of her new grandson. I had given her the Polaroid camera a week ago, when she offhandedly mentioned to me that she was feeling down about the fact that she had left all her most precious family photographs behind when they were forced to move to the camp. I happened to have brought an old Polaroid camera with me in my luggage, thinking to take photos of the conditions of the camp as part of my report back with the NATO team coordinators. But as soon as Saba had told me her woes, I knew she was in much greater need for the camera than I was, especially with the new baby on the way. Besides, there's a digital camera in everything nowadays.

Saba was gushing about her grandson so quickly I could hardly follow her words, having only a rudi-mentary grasp of the Pashto language, and for some reason my eyes flitted away to my left, staring over the heads of the bustling crowds, to land on the most startlingly handsome man I had ever seen.

Adrian O'Connor. High-ranking Navy SEAL, Smooth-talking American with dark, sandy-blond hair, vivid green eyes, impressive muscles, towering height, and a glorious ruddy tan. Of course, I didn't know his name yet at that moment. All I knew was that he was impossibly attractive. Blisteringly sexy. And looking right at me.

"*Bakhena gwaarum*, Saba," I said, patting her hand and excusing myself from the conversation. I would make it up to her later by purchasing one of her hand-spun pashmina scarves, but at that instant, I couldn't help myself. I was drawn to the handsome green-eyed soldier by an almost magical attraction, like he had cast a spell on me from all the way across the bazaar.

I pushed through the crowd like I was walking in a dream, my feet barely seeming to touch the dusty earth beneath me as I came closer and closer. But when I got to the other side of the congregation, he was nowhere to be seen. Like he had simply vanished into thin air.

Suddenly, I felt like an idiot. I wasn't there in the desert to lust after hot American boys. I was there to work. So I had returned to Saba's fabric stand with my tail between my legs to buy a scarf and listen dutifully as she rambled about how handsome and strong her new grandson was, proudly showing me Polaroids of the little baby.

As I sit here now in the hotel room, humming softly to Adrian, I think back to our second encounter, when I was standing at his tent, awaiting his return so I could give him the manila folder of classified information. When he was terribly late for our meeting. When he rolled up blasting his country music, sauntering up to me like some old-timey movie hunk. We had exchanged only a few words that day, as I was both too frustrated at being kept waiting and too flustered by the fact that this was the man I saw at the marketplace that day to really talk. Besides, I had promised myself to stay focused, not to let some hot shot American soldier knock me off my game. I was a NATO official, for god's sake, not a love-struck teenybopper.

But still, I couldn't get him off my mind.

And later that night, I was so burned out on trying to stay on the ball and overwhelmed with work that I decided to hit a local watering hole frequented by a lot of the NATO folks and soldiers alike. It was one of the few places in the country where soldiers had somewhere to go off-base. Drinking alcohol was an illegal activity with a terrible punishment for the locals, but that didn't stop them from using the presence of foreigners to make a profit. I could hardly blame them for it. Procuring booze for the stressed-out soldiers was one hell of a way to make some cash. I sat at the bar nursing my whiskey and going over some recent reports, my thoughts ricocheting uselessly in every direction as I tried all kinds of mental gymnastics to avoid thinking about Adrian O'Connor.

But it was impossible. He was there, in my mind.

He had somehow gotten under my skin, into my very veins. I couldn't stop recalling his handsome face, his alluring swagger, his impressive height. And then, almost as though I had summoned him with my thoughts, he walked through the door to the bar and strolled up to the counter. Right next to me.

He ordered straight gin and sat down on the stool beside me, then cast me a sidelong grin.

"Didn't expect to see you here," he said, that sexy Midwestern drawl that was like sweet molasses to my ears. I blushed instantly and took a quick swig of my drink, my face souring at the taste.

He laughed. "That bad, huh?"

"I don't usually drink," I replied, shrugging. I was too afraid to make eye contact with him, knowing that if I were to meet his vivid green eyes, I might be lost forever.

"So, then what's an innocent soul like you doing in a place like this?" Adrian asked, and maybe it was the liquid courage coursing through my veins, or maybe it was just happenstance, but I instinctively looked up at him before I could stop myself.

And from there, I was a goner.

We exchanged so few words but so many at the same time, conversation and confession flowed between us so easily. Before long, we were stumbling back to his private tent, our lips locked in a passionate, sloppy kiss. We fell into the blankets together, our limbs entangled, both of us moaning and crying out for each other. We made love fast and hard, our pent-up frustrations fueling every thrust and groan. We fucked once, then twice, and then a third time just before dawn. Exhausted and spent, we lay there in the cool early morning air, finally talking with our words instead of with our bodies. He told me where he was from, and I did the same. We talked about our fears, our hopes, our desires for the future. I felt, for the first time, like maybe we had a real connection that went far beyond the physical. We could have been something, if only we were in a different place, at a different time. But that desert was our Casablanca. It was all we had to share. And when six o'clock rolled around, we piled into his vehicle and he drove me back to my own barracks, where we said goodbye, not realizing it would be a real farewell.

Because later that day, while I was still drifting around on cloud nine, he was reassigned to a new location, a new battle. And so he was gone, just like that.

In my lap, Adrian is snoring lightly, his eyes closed. I smile down at him, realizing suddenly that there are tears in my eyes. It hits me just how bizarre it is. How impossible, that we should find each other again like this. I can't believe that our one night together in Afghanistan was enough to change both of our lives completely. After a few weeks passed in the desert, I was still in a funk, unable to forget about Adrian. He plagued my every waking thought as well as my wildest dreams. I couldn't believe he had slipped through my fingers so easily, so quickly.

I started feeling sick every morning when I woke up, and at first I assumed it was just heartache after spending the whole night dreaming blissfully that Adrian was still with me. But when I started actually vomiting every single morning, another explanation occurred to me, one that would entirely reroute the course I had planned out for my life.

I took a test, awkwardly waiting those three painstaking minutes in the barracks' communal bathroom, hoping nobody would walk in and see me that way. And when the three minutes were up, I checked the little window... and saw a tiny blue plus sign, clear as day.

I was pregnant.

For weeks, I tried to keep the news to myself, half out of fear that I would lose the position I had worked so tirelessly for, and half out of a sense of personal denial. I felt like a failure, like I had screwed everything up. I was pregnant with a child fathered by a man I hardly knew, after one admittedly magical one-night stand in the desert. But before too long, people started to take notice. Saba was one of the first to say something. One day when I was visiting her at the bazaar, she pointed to my belly, and in muted Pashto she asked, "Does anybody know yet?"

I wasn't even starting to show at that point, but Saba knew instinctively that there was something off about me. And in that moment, my heart sank. I realized that I was being a fool. There was no way I could go on hiding the truth like that. So, after psyching myself up for what I knew would be one of the hardest decisions I would ever make, I went to my superiors and informed them that I was pregnant and I needed to return home. They took it surprisingly well, and I was lucky enough to leave service with a hefty award of commendation for my efforts.

And from there, I had been living a totally different life. I lived with my parents again in rural Ontario, and when I gave birth, I was amazed and a little saddened to see that my beautiful baby daughter had bright, vivid green eyes.

Just like her handsome, mysterious father.

I gaze down at Adrian, my own eyelids growing heavy with exhaustion. It's been a rollercoaster of emotions these past couple of days, and I am more than ready to sleep, too. So I carefully scoot backward just enough to grab a pillow and position it between my head and the side of the bed, close my eyes, and fall asleep.

In the morning, I wake to find that I am no longer sitting on the floor with Adrian's head in my lap. Instead, I am lying in bed, the sheets lovingly pulled up to my chest. And there is the sound of whistling, accompanied by the delicious smell of bacon and eggs. I sit up slowly, yawning, and look over to see Adrian frying up breakfast in the little kitchenette area of our hotel suite. He's whistling to himself. Another song by Joseph Castello. I smile and start to get out of bed, but then Adrian looks up and shakes his head.

"Nope, you're not allowed to get up. How can I bring you breakfast in bed if you're not in bed?" he laughs, holding up a greasy spatula. I giggle and settle back into the sheets dutifully.

"Oh, you don't have to do that," I tell him, amused.

"Yeah, I do. It's the least I can do to thank you for helping me out last night. Those fireworks — well, they kind of took me back, you know. And not in a good way. I guess I should get used to that now, Canada Day and all. I forgot you were ahead of cele-bratory schedule up here. Anyway, thank you," he says, smiling at me.

I'm seeing a totally different side of him that I only caught a brief glimpse of back in the desert. When I first met him, I assumed he was just as cocky and womanizing as his fellow SEALs. Those boys were made for hard work and hard play, but there was nothing soft about them. Ever. But this man... this gorgeous, whistling prince charming of a man cooking me scrambled eggs and bacon in the kitchen... Well, he is a different breed altogether.

And suddenly, I know that he is safe. That I am safer with him than I have ever been.

And if that is true, then I know what I have to do now. I have to be honest with him.

So when he comes over to bring me a lovely plate of breakfast, I ask him to sit down on the bed with me. He regards me thoughtfully, those beautiful eyes full of an emotional depth I never expected to see there.

"So, there's something I need to tell you," I begin quietly, my heart pounding in my chest. "And I'm a little afraid of how you'll react, but I just can't hide it any longer, Adrian."

He cocks his head to one side slightly and asks, "What is it? Are you okay?"

I give him a reassuring smile and nod. "Yeah, yeah, I'm fine. But um, I just can't keep this secret anymore. It's not fair to you — or to Maya."

"What's going on, Bex?" he says, reaching over to take my hand.

I bite my lip, the words ready to burst from my throat.

"Maya is your daughter."

The world around me feels like it's falling silent as I drink in the words Becca tells me, those gorgeous, shining eyes watching me with such a mix of emotions I can't come close to interpreting.

Yet the silence around me isn't the tense, hellish silence I remember on the battlefield in Syria after a gunshot nearly deafened me. It isn't the same kind of silence I felt in those moments before the Russians stormed into the room to start a firefight. This is something altogether different.

My child. My own flesh and blood. Almost a year old.

I say nothing to Becca, just looking at her face for several long moments before I step away and turn my back on her, moving slowly into the bathroom to the crystal-clear mirror that reflects my image perfectly.

I hear Becca climbing out of bed and padding after me, and when she speaks, I can hear the terrified tenor in her voice, shaking.

"I'm so sorry, Adrian, I should have told you sooner!" she gushes, trying to hold back tears as I look at myself. "You have no idea how much I wrestled with the idea of whether or not to tell you, to explain what was going on in my life, all of it."

I say nothing, so she keeps speaking after a moment's hesitation, possibly wondering whether I was even hearing what she was saying, but it was quite the contrary: I caught every syllable that came out of her mouth.

"Adrian, please, all I'm asking is that you hear me out, just understand where I was coming from on this," she says, hardly able to keep up with her own words. "Everything I did, all I've been able to think about has been protecting my child. *Our* child, Adrian. I had to make sure everything I was doing was the right thing, and to do that, I had to be cautious. Every step of the way, even if that meant…"

She pauses, sniffing and wiping a tear from her eye. "Even if that meant hiding her from you, Adrian. But it wasn't because I don't think you're not going to be an incredible father, Adrian, please don't think that crossed my mind for a second!

"After everything I saw overseas, all the fighting, all the death, all the mayhem, after everything I went through, I couldn't just go on without taking precautions. I had to be careful with the most precious thing in my life, and I still am. I need you to understand, Adrian, please forgive me."

When I don't answer, I can almost feel her chest tightening, her jaw clenching as she searches for the right words to say, if there even are such things.

"I may have been overprotective. I don't know. Maybe I was right in what I did, maybe I wasn't. I… I don't know, Adrian," she sobs. "All I know is that I'm trying to make it right. I understand if you're mad, but please, look at it from my point of view. I'm sorry."

But the whole time she's talking, it's like she's muffled in the background to the thoughts that are swimming around furiously in my head. It's like a swelling storm spilling over into every part of my being.

And it feels ecstatic.

Everything about the past two years makes so much more sense now. It's like some missing piece of a puzzle that's been eluding me all this time has finally fallen right into my hands, and my chest swells so sweetly that I feel like I could walk on clouds.

It's exhilarating. I get it now. When I left for the field, when I was pulled away from Becca for some time, I felt like I'd left a piece of myself behind, like there was something tethering me to Becca and her life back here. I always thought it was something approaching love that I felt for Becca.

If I'm honest, that might still be a big part of it.

But now I understand why that feeling was so strong. It was her child. *Our* child. I feel my heart pounding fiercely and proudly in my chest, the very core of my biological drive as a human feeling so fulfilled, so completed.

I'm a father, and I couldn't be happier.

Even when I was in the middle of combat, going through the most intensive hell on earth that I could possibly experience, there was something very real tying me back to my home, the home that *is* Becca and our kid.

This feels so right, and it makes so much sense that my head is nearly dizzy. This is why I've felt her at my side in my darkest hours, this is why I've heard her soft voice whispering to me in the bleakest nights of my service to the country.

A world away from Becca, there was something tying us together all along, something pulling us to one another over insurmountable odds, and I knew my instincts were right without being able to place exactly why. But now I know.

And here she thinks *she* did something wrong?

I turn around suddenly, feeling a newfound energy in my chest, and I'm shocked to see fear in Becca's eyes. Real, profound fear of losing me, of anxiety over everything that she's just spilled out.

She flinches away, uncertain of what I'm going to do.

Was that the impulse that made her hide the child from me? Maybe some men would be angry, but I feel a mix of emotions. To some degree, I do feel a sting of disappointment from the one person I hoped to be nothing but understanding and trusting with me when I returned.

But her words haven't fallen on deaf ears. She's done everything to protect our child. Wouldn't I have done the same to make sure the most important thing in my life was going to be shared by capable, trustworthy hands?

And besides, I'm too overwhelmed by the joy of the revelation to feel anything approaching anger.

"Don't apologize, Becca," I say, taking her hands in mine calmly as she looks up at me uncertainly. Now it's my turn to comfort her. "There's no need for that."

"What?"

"I understand what you had to do," I say, giving her hands a gentle squeeze as she sniffs back tears. "It's not something that comes easily, and I know it must have been something you labored over for a long time."

I look back out the window for a moment and my blood is racing less fiercely, mellowed out by everything I've been feeling the past few minutes.

"I know more than anyone else how much life

out there can change you," I say, looking at her significantly. "That work you did isn't something you come out of without scars. Neither is SEAL service. Nobody knows that better than me — and now you too," I admit with a smile, and she manages one too through her tearstained eyes.

"Becca, I couldn't hold anything against you if I wanted to," I say, my deep voice a reassuring intonation to her. "You mean the world to me, you have ever since we parted ways. Don't think that doing what you felt you needed to do should be a hurdle to that."

"Are you sure you're okay with that, Adrian?" she says, gnawing her lower lip as she lets me pull her in closer. "I know you've been through a lot tonight, but-"

"If there's one thing I've learned from service, staying out in the wilderness with my comrades for months on end," I say with a sincere smile, "it's that I can't hold my feelings back."

She smiles, her eyes still teary, and I pick her up, swinging her around in a hug that makes her giggle. I walk her back to the bed and set her down, carefully moving the breakfast tray aside, and then I bring my lips to hers, kissing her in a deep, liberating exchange that makes my heart roar in bliss.

When it breaks, I smile at her, rubbing her back gently.

"It'll be okay, Becca. I know we both have some

healing to do, but I want to do it together or not at all."

"Me too," she says softly, losing herself in my eyes. I'm already gone in hers.

"Nothing's ever going to hurt our family as long as I'm alive, Becca," I say, my voice a little more serious now. I know I have enemies, but I'll wade through their bodies before I let anyone threaten what I've built with Becca after all this time, what little it is. It's the most valuable thing I've got. I smile. "But first things first."

"What's that?" she asks, tilting her head to the side.

I grin, taking her hips and pulling her into my lap as I lean back against the backboard of the bed, playing with her hair thoughtfully. "Tell me *every-thing* about our daughter. I've got a year to catch up on, after all."

We laugh in joy, but something bothers me. Not her. Not any of this. It's like when you feel the air change around you as dark storm clouds gather just along the horizon.

It's too good to be true. Something's not right.

I have a good feeling for these things.

I am ecstatic.

This morning it feels as though I'm walking on air — no, like I'm *dancing* on air. I feel weightless, buoyant, like a vibrant rose petal being gently lifted and carried about on a pleasant breeze. The weight of my dishonesty has finally been swept away from my shoulders and at last I feel like I can walk around with my head held high, my shoulders straight. I haven't been this happy since, well, since the day my daughter was born. And now she will have a father! Her *real* father!

All these confusing, complicated months of watching my baby girl grow up with a mingled sense of joy and regret are over. I mean, my little Maya already has a pretty strong male influence in her life in the form of her grandfather, my endlessly patient and steadfast dad. Between my parents and me,

Maya has wanted for very little in her days on earth thus far. I am an only child, and my parents had me when they were already in their late thirties, so there was pretty much no hope for them to ever give me a sibling. And I think they were getting a little bored and lonely while I was gone away working for NATO. I was their shining star growing up, the center of their universe.

So now they are overjoyed to have another little girl to spoil and adore. I have been incredibly lucky to have my parents around to help raise my daughter. They have taught her things that I never would have even thought of. For instance, my Quebecois mother speaks fluent French. My own handle of the language is… well, shaky, to say the least. But Maya's first word was actually *un toutou*, as she pointed excitedly at my father's cocker spaniel, Mitzy. It's moments like that which make me even more grateful to my parents for helping me raise my daughter.

But today I am over the moon at the thought of yet another wonderful person being added to the community of people taking care of Maya: her biological father, Adrian. Part of me is still in a state of shock and disbelief over how positively he reacted to my magnanimous revelation. I mean, it's kind of a big deal to suddenly learn that one has a secret child out there in the world. I am amazed and filled with gratitude that he responded so well to the news. I expected him to be angry. No, I expected him to be *furious*, really.

I'm still kicking myself over the fact that I kept my daughter hidden away from her father all this time. But I have to remind myself that I didn't do it for selfish reasons. It wasn't for my sake — it was for what I thought was my daughter's well-being. I assumed that her father would be vengeful and try to steal her away from me, from my parents, from everything she's ever known, in some long, drawn-out custody battle that would traumatize us all. Or even worse — I knew there was a chance that Adrian would simply want nothing to do with her, and my little girl would have to grow up knowing that her own father rejected her. But that was all fear talking in my mind. I knew Adrian better than that, even from our brief time together and the communication after.

Just the thought of that makes a lump rise in my throat. I think back on how wonderful it was to have my own father around all the time when I was growing up, and I can't imagine how empty Maya's life would be without the same kind of steady, protective influence. And even though Adrian has his issues — I mean, his past clearly still haunts him occasionally— I am confident that Maya will be much better off with her daddy around.

And then, of course, there's the fact that *I* want him around. For me.

Because even in this brief, tiny little window of time we've spent together, it has become increasingly obvious to me that Adrian is meant for me. We are cut from the same cloth, despite our apparent differences. We complete and complement each other in so many ways. I can feel myself beginning to really, truly fall for him.

How poetic, and how strange. We're doing it all backwards. It's supposed to be this way: date, fall in love, get married, have a baby. But I feel like we have the sequence all jumbled up, and now I have no idea what could be coming up next. Even stranger still, I don't even really mind not knowing. I am content to simply hop on this magical ride and see where it takes us. As long as we're together, I don't particularly mind where we end up or what we have to go through to get there.

Adrian and I have been cuddling in our lush, silken hotel bed, just dozing on and off, waking up now and again to kiss and gaze into each other's eyes. It feels like we are on our honeymoon, even though we aren't even married. Or engaged. But here in this bustling city, we have finally found a momentary oasis, a soft and pleasant spot where we can focus on nothing but each other.

Around nine o'clock, he sighs contentedly and wraps an arm around me, tugging me close so he can kiss my forehead. I giggle and press into his warm chest, breathing in his sweet, but manly scent.

"I could easily stay here all day like this," he says, his voice deep and husky.

I kiss his collarbone, running my fingers along his bulging bicep absentmindedly.

"Me, too," I reply. Adrian squeezes me tight and strokes my hair.

"But I think we should get up and take a quick shower. Then maybe head into town. I have something I want to shop for," he tells me, a little cryptically. I am almost too enraptured by the thought of taking a shower together to even question what he wants to go out looking for. But then I shake myself back to the present moment and force myself to ask.

"You? Shopping?" I say dubiously, grinning up at him. "What do you mean?"

"Well, it's shopping for you, really." He pauses, and I look at him expectantly. His sensuous lips crack into a broad grin and he continues, "I think it's time I put a ring on your finger, don't you?"

My heart does what feels like a complicated gymnastics move in my chest.

"Wh-what?" I splutter, totally blindsided. Like I said, our sequence is all jumbled up.

"I mean, I know what I want. And we already have a baby together, Bex. It seems only appropriate that we make this thing official. You are everything I've ever wanted, and I'll be damned if I let you slip through my fingers ever again," Adrian explains, cupping my cheek in his huge, calloused hand. My lips fall open as I struggle to come to terms with this new development.

"So, what do you say? Will you do me the honor of being my wife?" he presses on, still grinning at me with that gorgeous, cocky smile. I am reminded of him the way I first saw him, riding too fast and too dangerously up and down the Afghan dunes in that beat-up car, reckless and carefree even though I knew deep down he was strictly disciplined and in control. There is a kind of windswept charisma about him, his every smile or wink infused with a hint of adventure. I get the sense that a life by his side will be an exhilarating one. And it's a life I simply cannot pass up.

"Of course I will," I answer, laughing a little. "But aren't you supposed to be down on one knee or something?"

"Well, you and I have already broken with tradition in about a thousand other ways, but if you want me down on my knee, you got it!" he replies, getting out of bed and kneeling down. I giggle and scoot to the edge of the bed, looking down at the impossibly handsome man before me, offering me his empty hand.

When my eyes land on his open palm he says, "See? This is what I need to go shopping for. I can't properly propose to you until there's a ring in this hand. And I don't want to wait a minute longer to make you mine." He stands up and reaches down to sweep me up into his arms, causing me to squeal with delight and surprise.

"Where are you taking me?" I laugh, batting at his arm playfully.

"I told you! Quick shower, then it's off to put a ring on your finger," he responds with a wink.

My whole body tingles at the prospect of getting in the shower with him. Feeling his hard, powerful body slick and wet against my own. I gulp back my anticipation as Adrian carries me through the doorway to the ritzy hotel bathroom, with its high ceilings and glossy finishes. He sets me down gently and strips out of his t-shirt and boxers. I have to stifle a gasp, amazed to see him in this bright, exposing light. For a moment I am overcome with insecurity, realizing that now I will be totally vulnerable under the unforgiving fluorescent bulbs, too. Especially because the shower is essentially a giant rectangular cell with fully transparent glass walls, reflected clearly in the massive mirror on the opposite wall over the white marble sinks. I'll be totally exposed, and even though I have already been naked with Adrian before, this feels different. We're not being quick and hasty this time, and we're not fucking in the low light of evening. This is bright light. He will be able to see every line and curve of my post-baby body now.

Adrian turns on the shower and steps through the glass door, beckoning for me to strip down and follow. "Come on," he says, "I want to see all of your beautiful body."

I hesitate, biting my lip as I self-consciously fidget with the hem of my oversized t-shirt — one of his that I snuggled into sometime last night. But with him watching me expectantly, I know I can't deny him what he asks for. So I gingerly peel off the shirt and my little pink panties, tossing both aside as I unsuccessfully try to cover up my exposed parts with my hands.

Adrian gives me a confused look.

"Why are you hiding yourself from me? Bex, I've already seen you naked. You know I love every part of you."

I sigh and step into the shower with him, trying not to focus on how vulnerable I feel now. Adrian quickly pulls me into his arms and strokes the dampening hair back from my face, peering down at me fondly. As he slowly runs his fingertips down my neck, my arms, my curvy waist, I start to relax. Adrian knows me. He has known me since the moment we locked eyes at the bazaar. There is no reason for me to shy away from him. We are meant to be, and the one place I should feel most comfortable and free is in his arms.

He gently tips my chin upward to kiss me deeply, his tongue probing at my lips. I open my mouth to give him access, all but melting into his warmth, his incredible strength. He can bend me and mold me so easily, like I'm just a lump of obedient clay in his hands. Adrian knows just how to turn me on, how to make me tick. His hands slide down my back to grip my ass, pulling me closer to him so that his hard, stiff cock pokes into my thigh. He moans into our kiss, one of his hands roving up to caress my breast, his thumb trailing circles over my nipple. Tiny pinpricks of pleasure shoot down my body and I lean into his touch hungrily. I have longed for this. I find myself craving Adrian in a way I never expected to, like he's a drug I never want to quit.

He begins to grind against me slightly, his shaft sliding back and forth across my thigh. I can feel myself getting slick between the thighs, and not from the shower water running down my back. Everything is soft and steamy, our bodies pressed so closely together I can hardly tell where my body ends and his begins. We are one, moving united under the deliciously warm water.

Adrian reaches down to cup my tingling sex and I gasp as he plants a biting, insistent kiss along the slope of my neck, sucking at my skin until a rosy mark blooms there. His fingers expertly stroke my clit, flicking along my wet opening as I rock into his hand, needing more, more, more.

"Oh god," I whisper, closing my eyes and giving in to the sensation. Adrian groans, clearly pleased with himself. He slips a finger inside me and I cry out, nearly falling over at the sudden penetration, but he catches me and holds me still. We kiss sloppily, the shower spray wetting our faces as Adrian pumps his finger in and out of my aching pussy.

"It feels so fucking good," I groan, clutching at his shoulders as my pleasure mounts ever higher and higher, until finally an orgasm shatters over me, my legs trembling and my knees buckling beneath me. But Adrian holds me up, lifting his hand to suck my juices from his finger. He turns me around so that his cock presses against my ass cheek, rutting against me.

"Bend over for me, baby," he orders softly, his voice rough and raspy with need. I can tell he's doing everything possible to hold back, to take it slow. But I don't want that — I want him to use me, to fill me up and lose control.

"Whatever you want, you can have," I tell him plainly as I bend over, spreading my legs wider. He lets out a low groan of approval, his huge hands squeezing my ass, pushing them apart and sliding his cock along my slick cunt. That sensation in itself is nearly orgasmic and I back up into him greedily.

"I've dreamt about this for so long, Bex," he tells me, slapping my ass. I can tell he's getting closer to losing control. I want him to take me, hard, fast, however he desires.

"Me too," I answer breathlessly. "Take me, Adrian. Please. I need it."

"I wanted to be slow and gentle for you, baby, but

you're making it hard for me," Adrian replies, and the catch in his voice tells me he really is struggling. "I just want to ram that sweet little cunt, fill you up with my seed. I want to put another baby inside you so badly, Bex."

I whimper with need. I want the same thing. I want him to fuck me hard, to give in to his primal desire to spread his seed. "Please, Adrian. Give it to me. I want you to use me. Fuck me."

That does the trick. He grasps my hip and guides the head of his engorged shaft into my slick opening, my vaginal walls shuddering at his entrance. He sheaths himself inside me completely, until I am aching with fullness. He doesn't even attempt to go slowly anymore. His gentleness disappears, replaced by an animalistic rhythm, thrusting wildly into my cunt. The tip of his glorious cock slams into my g-spot again and again, making me cry out with ecstasy. He leans over and slides his hands along my waist, over my belly, and upward to caress my breasts as he pummels into me, his fingers tweaking and stroking my nipples so that I'm very close to dangerous overstimulation. It's too much. All at once. But I can't bring myself to ask him to stop, and I know deep down that I don't want him to.

"You make me feel so damn good, Bex. You're perfect," he whispers. Tears of pleasure burn in my eyes and I struggle to reply.

"Oh god… fuck me, Adrian," I manage to

whimper softly, reaching out to brace myself against the steamy shower wall, my hand making a slippery print on the glass.

"I want you to come for me, baby. I want to feel you fall apart all around me," Adrian commands, squeezing my breasts as he quickens the pace of his thrusts. And just like that, I can feel my pussy seizing up, my whole body tensing in preparation for the big release. Almost like he has total control over me, over what I feel.

It's bizarre — we barely know each other, yet one could nearly believe we've known each other for years, we're so in sync. So connected.

"Come for me, sweetheart," he growls, and my body obeys.

"Oh my god!" I cry out as first one, then a second orgasm comes barreling through me, my cunt twitching and convulsing with ecstasy. My legs buckle beneath me and I start to collapse, my head feeling faint and dizzy. But Adrian supports me, his muscular arms more than enough to keep me up while he continues to plow into my pussy from behind, his heavy balls slapping against me wetly.

"Fill me up, Adrian, please. Give it to me. I need it," I moan wantonly, bucking backward against him for encouragement. I'm desperate for it now— I need to feel his precious cream spurting inside of me. I need to feel him use me like the breeder I am.

"Anything for you," he groans, and as he grasps

my hips, he bellows out my name and releases a thick stream of his seed deep within me. I instinctively clench my pussy, trying to hold onto his cum as long as I can. I can't deny it — I want nothing more than for Adrian to fill me with his virility, mark me forever as his own.

Adrian gently wraps his arms around me and turns me back around to face him, stroking my wet tendrils of dark hair back from my temples as he kisses me softly, our bodies pressed together as his seed slowly drips down my thigh. I let out a breathless little laugh, so exhilarated with the way we can both just let go of any sense of self-consciousness and lose control… together. I've never felt so free and comfortable with anyone before. Gone is my impulse to hide myself, to cover up. Gone is my shame and nervousness, replaced by warmth and calm.

"Here, let me wash you off," he murmurs sweetly, smiling down into my face. He reaches for the luxurious hotel soap, some expensive brand I've never used before, and starts to lather my body. His hands, once gripping and insistent, are now so soft and tender, sliding lovingly over my every curve. He grabs the detachable shower head and rinses me off, then starts to wash my hair.

I've never had anyone but me wash my hair — well, except for the occasional hair dresser, of course — and certainly never in such an intimate fashion. Normally,

I consider myself a pretty independent person. I do my best to support myself and never ask for help. I can look out for myself and my family without anyone to be my crutch. But there's something about Adrian. Perhaps it's the reservoir of incredible strength and power he keeps dutifully restrained, coupled with his immense capacity for tenderness… I just can't resist. I don't feel infantilized or condescended to when he calls me "baby" or "sweetheart" or when he carries me around so easily like I'm just a ragdoll. I know he respects me, he understands my own strengths, and I know deep down with a doubt that he will never cross any line I draw out for him.

Adrian knows my vulnerabilities, but he doesn't hold them against me. He senses what I want, what I need, without my having to say a single word.

So I simply close my eyes and give into the delicious sensation of having someone else take care of me. His surprising tenderness is such a sharp contrast to the way he fucks me, all raw passion and unrestrained force. There are many sides to this man, I'm learning, and I am eager to acquaint myself with every single one.

After we finish showering, we dry off and get dressed, preparing to head out into town for lunch and to start ring shopping. I'm nearly tingling with excitement, I'm so giddy. Once again, I'm walking on air. It's hard to believe that just a few days ago I was bored and lonely in my Mississauga hotel room, waiting for the next frantic, paranoid call from my client. To his credit, the poor guy has only left three voicemails on my phone in the past couple days. As I strap on my wedge sandals, I'm holding my cell phone between my shoulder and my ear, finally calling the guy back.

He answers fervently, "Ms. Summers?"

"Yes, hello, Mr. Green. I'm here. Sorry I missed your calls — it's been a busy couple of days here. Is everything okay? The system working out?" I reply, trying to make my voice sound as genuinely concerned as possible while also rolling my eyes at Adrian.

"You wouldn't pick up and I was starting to worry—"

"Yes, I apologize. Like I said, I was preoccupied. But I'm here now."

"—it's just unnerving to get your voicemail so many times in a row—"

"Mr. Green, is there a problem?" I interrupt again, enunciating more clearly. He finally stops chattering nervously and sighs.

"Well, no. Not really. There was a moment where I thought one of my new g-guards was spying on my w-wife in the shower, but I think I was just being paranoid," he splutters. I have to stifle a laugh. I feel quite confident that none of my personally-hired-

and-vetted security guys would risk his job to peep on someone.

"I can assure you that no such thing will happen. Not on my watch," I tell him, grateful that he can't see me grinning on the other end of the line. "My men are superbly trained and disciplined. I promise you there's no need to worry. Now, I will be heading back home soon, so if there's anything else you need, please understand that I will not be readily available. My contract with you ended yesterday, remember?"

There's a long pause. Then he goes on, in a rather defeated tone, "Yes, I know. But I was wondering, um, maybe you would like to g-get dinner some-time?" His voice perks up toward the end and my mouth falls open in surprise. Adrian gives me a confused look and I shake my head.

"Mr. Green, you are married. You just mentioned your wife to me. I have met her. We had a lovely luncheon meeting together, all three of us, you'll recall?" I tell him slowly, totally shocked.

I can nearly feel the regret in his voice when he replies, "Oh, um, yes. You're right. Totally out of line for me to ask that. Terribly sorry— uh, um, well— I will send your check in the mail posthaste. Th-thank you very much for your work, and ah, have a wonderful day!"

Click. I stare at the phone in disbelief for a moment.

"What? What did he say?" Adrian asks curiously.

"The married bastard just tried to ask me out!" I laugh, shaking my head.

"Well, I can hardly blame him. I mean, look at you," Adrian replies, shrugging. He kisses the back of my hand and then says, "Come along, my love! I'm starving, and I can't wait to get started on the ring hunt!"

The two of us head out to the *Café Crepe* in the middle of the Toronto hubbub, where we get an outside table so we can listen to the birds chirping as they flit along from one perfectly-manicured topiary to the next. This is the kind of charming restaurant I rarely went to anymore, now that I have a tempestuous little girl with me almost all the time. Suddenly, my heart pangs with longing, and a rush of fondness for Maya takes over me. I miss her. This is one of the longest times I've spent away from her since she was born, and it's difficult. Of course, having the massive distraction of Adrian looking right at me is definitely helping the situation.

The waitress takes our order — an extra spicy Bloody Mary and a Montreal Smoked Meat crepe for him, a mimosa and spiced pecan, apple and brie salad for me — and then flounces away, leaving us alone at our table together. Adrian folds his hands in front of him, looking at me with a kind of amused fascination.

"It's still hard to believe," he says softly. "All that time I spent dreaming about you, just wishing I could see you one more time... and now, here we are."

I smile at him. "I know. I feel the same way. It's almost overpowering, isn't it?"

Adrian nods and reaches across the table to take my hands, which are so small and fragile-looking next to his. "Bex, it's a good thing we came out here in public to talk, because if we were still alone together back in that hotel room... well, I can't promise we would be able to do much talking. It's all I can do not to swing you over my shoulder and make you mine. Again and again."

I can feel my cheeks flushing bright pink at this confession, especially because I feel exactly the same way. There's an animal attraction between us almost too strong to fight, but I know that we have serious matters to discuss— fully clothed.

"First of all, I think it's about time I see a photo of our daughter," he says, beaming proudly.

"That sounds wonderful," I reply, overjoyed. I scoot my chair around to sit beside him and take out my cell phone, pulling up the photo gallery and flipping through an almost endless album of baby pictures. Maya in her first professional photograph. Maya in her high chair with birthday cake smeared all over her face. Maya sleeping peacefully in a hammock strung between two old trees in my parents' woodsy backyard. Adrian is nearly speechless, and I can feel the downright adoration burning off of him as we coo and smile over pictures of our little girl.

Our food and drinks arrive and we continue chatting, with me sharing anecdotes and funny stories about Maya's first steps, her first word, the antics she's gotten into since learning how to crawl, and everything in my life seems to be perfectly aligned. For once. I feel utterly content and yet buzzing with excitement for the future. I can't wait for Adrian to meet his daughter. I can't wait to begin the next chapter of my life with the man of my dreams.

Still laughing at some comment Adrian made about Maya's hair sticking straight up in one of her baby pictures, I glance up and do a double take over his shoulder.

My smile fades as my instincts hone in on an individual down the street, perched on a motorcycle and dressed in gray leather, despite the warmth of summer. I squint, trying to see his face more clearly. Something about him unnerves me, puts me on edge.

Like I've seen him before.

And he's looking at me the same way.

"Okay, so...let's talk metals."

I smile and glance over at Becca as we start walking away from my car and heading into the lavish jewelry store downtown. It's a tall building with black, shining marble interiors and soft white lighting that makes every inch of the staggering wealth inside visible. We're ring shopping, and I won't accept anything but the very best for her.

"Let me guess, you're not a 'gold' kind of lady?" I say, holding the glass door open for her before stepping inside. I feel a number of heads turn to look at us as we walk in. That's partly because of the fact that we're obviously a young couple looking for a ring, but my height tends to have that effect on just about anyone.

"Well, it's just that you see yellow gold

everywhere," she says, smiling playfully as she eyes the rows of jewelry in glass display cases.

An attendant bustles up to us in a matter of seconds, but I hold him off with a look, and he nods respectfully, backing away. I want my girl to have her time to peruse before we let the salesmen start courting us.

We've dressed the part of what we're here for, too. Becca convinced me to put on a designer crimson button-down I still have. My muscles have grown since the last time I wore it, so it's a tight fit, but she seems to like it rolled up to the sleeves, my black pants showing off my powerful thighs as we walk.

As for her, she's been drawing eyes all day in a nearly matching red crop top, jeans that display those beautiful, long legs of hers, and a pair of heels that click as we peruse the store, a strappy white leather bag dangling off her shoulder. Her sleek hair spills down her shoulder and frames her face beautifully, accenting those gorgeous cheekbones that make for a breathtaking smile.

"Alright, so maybe white gold?" I suggest, stepping over to a dazzling display of rings in various shades and sizes, and I smile at the sight of her looking so awed by everything she sees.

"White gold's alright..." she trails off, and I roll my eyes.

"So what are you leading me to?"

She pauses in front of a small display of rose gold jewelry, and I raise an eyebrow. "Rose gold? Didn't think you were the type, but I like it."

"Hold on, 'type?' Don't tell me you have an eye for jewelry," she says, grinning up at me, and I laugh a little.

"You'd be surprised what skills you pick up in the SEALs." In truth, one of my earliest operations had been shutting down a high-profile jewelry heist in Monaco to fund arms purchases by terrorists. Doing so had entailed learning everything there was to know about jewelry and its forgeries, but she doesn't need to know the gritty details. "My one request is that we don't do diamonds."

"Oh, thank god," she gushes, gliding around some of the other display cases and taking in the sights of huge rubies, shining topaz, and sparkling amethysts. "Everyone has them. I want my ring to be different."

That, and there's more blood behind the production of any given diamond than your average unmarked firearm, but that's not something I ought to bring up out loud in the middle of a jewelry store. By the look Becca and I exchange, I can tell that she's well aware of that herself. Her job had her dealing with the armed forces of just about every western nation, after all, up to their elbows in every kind of problem.

It's so strange, having the connection to someone like Becca that I do. Both of us are trying to put on this facade of a civilian life, but there's so much underlying it all that the people around us don't see. But Becca understands it — maybe not to the degree of what all there is to know about SEAL life, but it's something, and damn, does Becca ever make it sweet.

The thought of having her as a wife makes me swell both with pride and with lust. She's been through so much, so treating her to picking out whatever ring she desires feels all the more satisfying.

"I can't say they're my favorite either," I admit with a chuckle. "So what do you think, maybe a nice sapphire?" I show her over to a display of white sapphires that look quite a lot like diamonds to the untrained eye. But when you've had to dig through a Serbian mobster's suitcase to pick out one such a jewel, you don't forget what they look like.

"Oooh, that *is* pretty," she agrees, but I don't fail to notice her glancing sidelong at me with an incredulous smile at my competence in spotting jewels. "Rubies are nice, too, and the shade might complement the rose gold nicely."

"A pink ruby would be nice against the metal, too, if we're just going all-out with this nontraditional engagement ring," I suggest, and her eyes sparkle at that visual, her smile spreading even wider across her face. To my surprise, she slips her arms around my waist and hugs me as she looks down at all the displays, letting out a soft, contented sigh into my side.

"I think a nontraditional ring would be good for us," she says, her tone light-hearted as I give her hip a squeeze, wishing I had somewhere more private to take her; every moment we're together makes me want her more. "We're kind of a nontraditional pair, you know?"

"You've got a point," I laugh, finally gesturing to one of the attendants keeping their distance to come size her finger for us. But as the attendant hurries off to go get the necessary equipment, Becca turns up to me, a hint of worry in her eyes.

"The more I think about it, the more it feels like we're kind of working backwards in our relationship."

I tilt my head to the side, stroking her back and giving her an even gaze, trying to gauge her thoughts. "And how do you feel about that? Does that upset you? I know what you mean, I suppose— missing out on the fairy tale romance of falling in love, getting engaged, married, then having a kid. That we're not getting that."

She hesitates, chewing on her lip a moment, but it's not like trying to break bad news. Rather, she seems to be figuring out how to put the words together before speaking slowly.

"Maybe, a long time ago, there was a part of me that wanted that." She turns to face me, wrapping her small arms around my massive torso, not able to reach all the way behind me, but contenting herself to feel my rock-hard abdomen.

"But all that went out the window when I found out I was pregnant," she says, a smile lighting up that irresistible face again. "That life isn't for me. I haven't looked back ever since I became a mother. This stuff doesn't work out the way the movies try to sell it, and honestly… I'm so glad it's happening the way it is," she says, burying her face in my chest.

I lift her chin up and bend down to kiss her, feeling her heart flutter as I pull her in close to me, and for a moment, I forget the jewelry store is even around us, everything falling away except for the two of us.

We're interrupted by a store clerk clearing his throat, and I glance away to notice him standing behind the counter with a ring sizer, his lips pursed. I hold up a finger to instruct him to wait while I finish kissing the love of my life, something of a possessive rumble in my chest as she sighs into the kiss.

When we finally break, I look up at the clerk and give him a boyish smile. "Sorry man, I just got back from the Middle East. I get a little caught up in things now and then."

"Oh!" the man says, face reddening a bit from embarrassment, and he hurriedly smiles. "My apologies, sir. Welcome home — and thank you for your service." He gives a warm smile before tending to Becca's ring finger, and I stand at her side, watching the process.

I always have mixed emotions when people thank me for my service. Mostly because none of them, not one, ever knows what exactly they're thanking me for.

On the one hand, it's nice to know I'm appreciated back home. Knowing that civilians have my back is a quiet reassurance on a day to day basis. Even if I was serving the country south of the Canadian border.

On the other hand, it's frustrating.

I think back to the past two years, and how if I'd quit the service earlier in life, maybe I would have gotten the chance to give Becca the storybook romance she used to want. I know she's happy this way, but part of me nags at the back of my mind, wondering if she might have been even happier with a different start.

But there's so much more to it than that. Unbidden, my mind flits back to that night in Syria where something as simple as a little bad intelligence nearly cost my whole team their lives. While the clerk is discussing ring sizes with Becca, I'm zoning out, thinking back to the sight of my communications officer losing his life right in front of my eyes.

His name was Marco, and he was my best friend. We'd gone through training together when we were in the academy, before SEAL training was even an option for us.

I remember him talking about his own hopes and dreams for starting a family when he got out of the service. He wanted to settle down in a nice apartment in the city. We'd always disagreed about that — the idea of a metro apartment sounds like hell to me even to this day – but he was from the Bronx, and he wanted something that reminded him of his childhood, just like I did.

We all knew the risks of going into the service. It was something we went into each and every operation with. But that's so different from the reality of seeing your best friend gunned down in front of you by someone you weren't even expecting to have to fight in your wildest dreams.

Becca turns to look at me and ask my opinion about a certain metal, and I absent-mindedly say a few words about it, my thoughts still distracted.

Still, though, seeing Becca's face lit up by everything she's getting to do right now reminds me of the positives of how things have worked out.

One man died that night in Syria, but I wonder how many more might be dead right now if I hadn't been there. I was able to spring into action before anyone else, able to deal with those grenades and that ambush with unbeatable precision.

There was nothing about that night I thought I could have done better. I've been telling myself that for so long — I've had to, from the moment we finally made it to the helicopter that retrieved us for extraction. If it hadn't been me leading that operation, all those men might have been dead.

As well as a few Russians. They weren't expecting to go into that firefight, either. The only man I hold to blame is that commander who wouldn't back down. If he'd known when to admit the mistake, to cease firing and back off for negotiation, none of this would have happened. He'd still have all his men, as well as that eye I cost him.

I'm snapped from my thoughts as Becca finishes getting sized, and we discuss things with the clerk a little more — the kinds of metals we're interested in, what the pricing is going to be like, what kinds of designs we're interested in, and so on.

"...and we have a few models that might interest you, based on what I heard the two of you talking about earlier, if you don't mind my eavesdropping," the clerk says, disappearing behind the door for a few moments before emerging with a sample ring in hand that makes Becca's jaw drop. "But I think this is something special you'll appreciate."

He presents Becca with a lovely platinum ring set with a massive, blood-red ruby in an opal cut. On each side, it's flanked by smaller, circular gems, all of them glittering in the light of the jewelry store.

"A ruby flanked by smaller white sapphires, inlaid in that design in rose gold," I muse, nearly reading the salesman's mind. "You're trying to make this too easy for us, aren't you?"

I flash the clerk a grin, and he gives an embarrassed laugh back. I know he's just happy to show this off because it's undoubtedly one of the most expensive models in the store, easily many thousands of dollars. The thought of spending even more than that on Becca makes my heart race.

"It's gorgeous," Becca gushes, holding the ring up in her hands and imagining what it might look like to our specifications.

"We've got a few more shops to check out," I say, a nearly teasing grin on my face as I rub Becca's shoulders when she looks up at me in childlike hopefulness. "But I think this is a strong contender."

"Of course, this would be a custom design based on this model," the clerk says, putting away his prize gold mine. "So we'd need to go over specifics several weeks in advance of the actual purchase."

"I don't doubt it," I say confidently, my eyes still on Becca. "We'll be in touch."

"Certainly. Here's my card if you have any questions. Have a lovely day, both of you," the clerk says, beaming at us as I put my arm around Becca and lead her out of the store, her starry eyes suddenly looking around at the models in the store with newfound creativity in her mind.

We start heading down the road of the downtown thoroughfare when she practically hops up and down in excitement. "Oh my god, this is amazing! I've never felt like I've had so much creative power!"

I laugh out loud, my eyes scanning for the next jewelry store a few buildings down. "Take your time and enjoy it, then, it's something that's worth putting a lot of thought into!"

"It's almost overwhelming," she says, running her hand through her hair, but then she beams up at me. "I'm so glad you're as into this as I am! I can't imagine doing all this with someone who didn't care."

"Men who don't care about what their lovers get passionate about don't deserve to have their lovers," I say, slipping my hand around her narrow one as we walk.

As we stroll down the road, something catches my attention out of the corner of my eye, though I don't look in that direction. As a SEAL, I learned to pick up on certain irregularities in the environment around me. You're constantly scanning the vicinity for threats, even when you suppose yourself to be totally safe.

And something about the man watching us from across the street makes me feel anything but.

The man looks Russian by the look of him — Eastern European features and mannerisms get imprinted on your mind after so much time around them – and this guy fits the bill. His eyes are as blue as the sky, so vibrant as to be visible all the way across the street, and his hair is a silvery gray.

More interesting is his vehicle. He's perched on a motorcycle, a well maintained chopper that looks like it's got more effort put into it than your average motorist. To anyone else, he'd look like just another intimidating gang banger, but what I see in the man is something to be suspicious of.

Veterans fall into motorcycle gangs all the time. They come home disenfranchised, and they find some camaraderie they lack from civilians in the rough and liberty-loving bikers who blaze across the highways in patchy leather jackets.

And this guy seems like he's former military. There's a certain look that training gives you. It comes out in your resting posture, the way you carry yourself without noticing.

The way this Russian veteran is eyeing me doesn't sit well with me at all. I have to fight my instincts not to glare right back at him until he backs down, and I don't want to do that while Becca's at my side. Not while she's having the time of her life.

But I can't help but think back to the Russians I killed that night in Syria. I know one thing that's haunted the back of my mind ever since that night, ever since I took those Russian lives: my face mask was off when I fought those men.

And just as I remember the face of that damn Russian commander, his visage burned into my memory like a hot iron brand, I know that each and every one of the survivors of that night know my face.

As all that runs through my mind, I try to force the thoughts away. He's probably just some Russian biker hanging around downtown, maybe waiting for a meetup.

But even as we leave him behind and head into the next shop, which is twice as lavish and upscale as the first, I can't help but hear that nagging voice in the very back of my mind.

After all this time, has the war followed me home?

"It's so beautiful," I murmur aloud, shaking my head at the ring in my palm.

Well, actually, it's just a photo of the ring I took on my cell phone while we were in the upscale, celebrity-grade jewelry store earlier today. After hours of poring over different stones, metals, gemstone cuts, and carats and karats, we finally settled on a scintillating, super-gorgeous pale pink sapphire, coupled with a 24-karat white gold band. I decided on a princess cut for the gem, and Adrian insisted on adding a halo of tiny blue sapphires to encircle the pink gem, representative of Maya.

"Because," he explained, holding both my hands and gazing deeply into my eyes, "when I ask you to marry me, I know I am not just gaining the woman of my dreams, but the daughter I have always longed for, too. The pink sapphire is you, and the blue ones represent our little girl."

It is silly, maybe, to put so much stock in something as material as a ring. But I can't help but feel a rush of warmth as I stare at the photograph of what my engagement ring will look like. Adrian is holding my hand over the console while he drives us down the 401, leaving Toronto and heading back into the Ontario wilderness toward my parents' house in the country.

He glances over at me and smiles. "Well, no ring they can make will ever come close to how beautiful *you* are, but they can damn sure try," he says, squeezing my hand sweetly.

"Oh, stop. You can't spoil me like this, you know," I tell him, with mock seriousness. "Once we get to my parents' house and you meet my family, they'll set you straight. They live well out there, but I can tell you right now they're going to think we're being reckless and silly for getting engaged like this. And the ring... god. They're going to tell you off for spending so much money on me!"

"No, they won't," Adrian counters, laughing. "Bex, they're your parents. Surely they want whatever is best for you. Whatever makes you happy."

"Well, yeah, of course. But they just might have a different idea of what that means," I reply.

"Either way, don't you worry about any of it. If

there's one thing I'm good at, it's winning over people's families. Believe it or not, I can turn the whole cocky tough guy persona on and off at will," he assures me with a wink. I can't help but laugh out loud.

"No, you can't! My parents are gonna take one look at you and realize you're the guy they always warned me about. Tall, tough, with an attitude," I shoot back, poking my tongue out at him.

"Oh, come on. That's not what you think of me, is it?" he asks, still grinning.

"Okay, fine. I know you're more than that. You're… different, you know," I sigh.

"Different from what?"

"From what I thought you were at first," I answer honestly.

"Oh really?" Adrian says, raising both eyebrows. Now he's interested.

"Well, yeah. I mean, when I first met you I thought you were just some super attractive cocky playboy with a James Dean complex," I admit, giggling. Adrian shoots me a faux-offended look. "Oh, don't act like that's a surprise! Besides, I'm sure you thought badly of me at first, too!" I add.

He shakes his head, smiling more to himself than for my sake, like he's recalling a fond memory.

"No, Bex. I thought you were an angel," he replies, glancing over at me. The calm, female voice of the GPS instructs us to turn right. As the car veers off the highway and down a gravel, woodsy road, Adrian laughs softly.

"You remember what I said to you that day out in the desert?" he asks, an amused look on his impossibly handsome face.

"You asked me if I was a mirage," I answer, rolling my eyes good-naturedly. He nods.

"Yeah. It was a serious question," Adrian says. "I had been out driving around the desert for so long, just dunes of golden sand stretching out all around me for miles and miles — and it got me into some weird kind of funk. When I saw you standing there waiting for me... well, at first I could hardly believe you were real. In fact, sometimes even now I almost have to reach out and touch you just to make sure you're truly there."

My heart is fluttering wildly in my chest at his surprisingly vulnerable, romantic words.

I squeeze his hand, lifting it up so I can kiss it. "Oh yeah, you're definitely much more than I originally thought, Adrian. You never cease to surprise me."

"That's the goal," he responds flippantly, giving me a wink. Looking around at the lush greenery surrounding us, he sighs contentedly. "God, this place is beautiful. I mean, where I grew up in the Midwest I was more used to rolling plains than thick forest. And then the desert..."

"This is home," I reply, staring out the window at the huge, probably ancient trees, the thick underbrush. Out here in the Canadian woods, I can almost pretend I'm living out some prehistoric, garden of Eden-type fantasy. Just me and my handsome, powerful mate, trekking across the unspoiled landscape in search of adventure and romance.

Even though the wildlife is mostly hiding out during the day, we are approaching the evening hours, during which many of the animals come out to hunt and roam the woods. As we drive, the thick vegetation begins to clear out little by little until we reach one of my favorite places in the world — this gorgeous, barely-touched small lake in the middle of the forest. This land used to belong to my great-great-grandparents, who had once planned to use it as farmland, but who fell too deeply in love with the wild beauty of the place to bring themselves to destroy it. Since then, it was sold off, and the land is no longer owned by my family. But the company that bought it hasn't touched it yet, thank god, so this beautiful lake remains undisturbed.

"Oh wow," Adrian breathes, his eyes drinking the beauty laid out before us. Suddenly, a completely spontaneous and ridiculous idea occurs to me. Our past couple of days together have been a whirlwind of changes. I have seen a side of Adrian I never expected, and a side of myself I never acknowledged.

So what better time than this for some silly adventures?

"Pull over," I tell him, biting my lip excitedly. He gives me a confused look.

"Why? Are you okay?" he asks, furrowing his brow.

"Yeah, I'm perfect," I answer brightly. "I just think we should go for a quick swim, that's all."

"You mean… skinny dipping?" Adrian clarifies, looking amused but interested.

"Mhmm!"

"What are we, sixteen?" he teases. But he pulls over, just the same. My heartbeat quickens as I jump out of the car, peel off my clothes, toss them in the backseat, and bolt for the undoubtedly cool water of the pristine lake. I can hear Adrian laughing raucously from the car, but a moment later, he sheds his own clothing and follows after me, grinning widely.

I splash into the water, the breath catching in my throat at the sudden drop in temperature — but I push through the shivers. This is my idea, and I'm going to follow through!

"Jesus, this is cold!" Adrian exclaims, swearing under his breath as he wades in behind me, his arms outstretched. He comes up and captures me in a swift embrace, our lips meeting instantly. With his massive, powerful body pressed against me, I immediately feel quite a bit warmer, and I fold happily into his arms.

"You're a crazy person, you know that?" he murmurs, kissing the top of my head. I giggle, still shivering a little with the cold.

"I swear I don't normally do things like this," I assure him.

"I'm certainly not going to complain about it," he says, shrugging. "I happen to like this new, spontaneous version of Rebecca Summers. But to be fair, I really like every single version of you."

"I really like you, too," I answer, and I have to laugh out loud. We both sound like two high school kids confessing that they *"like like"* each other. We're not kids anymore, but god, I do feel so young and carefree and reckless when I'm with Adrian. He loosens the strict, disciplined chains that bind me to my responsibilities and worries. He shows me a different way of looking at the world. He sets me free.

"Well, then," Adrian begins, tilting my chin up so I'm looking right into his handsome face, "I think we should do something about that. Don't you?"

"What do you mean?" I ask innocently, batting my eyelashes. I know exactly what he means, but I can't resist egging him on, especially when we're this close together. There's nothing between us— no barriers, no fears, no clothing. Just two warm bodies pressed together in the middle of the wilderness, waist-deep in the water.

"I'll show you," he says, and the husky tone of his voice tells me exactly what is about to happen, before he even makes his first move. He leans down to kiss me deeply, his tongue probing into my mouth. I allow him access, pressing in more closely to his muscular frame. I can feel his hardening length straining against my upper thigh and I reach down to caress it. But at the sensation of his stiff, velvety-soft shaft hard against my fingertips, I can't pull back. I can't resist.

I wrap my fingers around his engorged cock and begin to slowly stroke him up and down, my thumb sliding along the sharply-sensitive ridge on the underside. Adrian groans into our kiss, sending a delicious thrum of vibrations down both of our bodies. I tighten my grasp ever so slightly, pumping his cock with one hand while the other cups the back of his neck.

Adrian's own hands rove down my shoulders and arms, then slide over to caress my breasts. I can feel my nipples stiffening under his gentle, careful ministrations, as spirals of pleasure spin through my core. I can feel myself getting wetter by the second, my pussy aching to have Adrian's glorious cock sheathed inside of me once again. I moan into his mouth, sliding my fingers up and down his shaft.

Without further ado, Adrian lifts me up and I

wrap my legs around his waist, his cock springing free of my grasp to press against my ass. With his arms braced around me, supporting me, he reclines me backward, my hair dragging the water's surface, so he can lean in and nip at my breasts. His tongue roams across my nipples, his teeth lightly grazing them with tiny pinpricks of pleasure. I whimper and tilt my head back, overwhelmed by the contrasting sensations of his warm mouth and arms with the cool water. Goosebumps rise up along my flesh and I give into Adrian's control, falling limp and pliable in his powerful arms. He can do whatever he wants with me — I belong to him. I have belonged to him ever since the first moment we laid eyes on each other in the crowd, from the first words he spoke to me, from the first time we touched at that desert bar.

He lifts me up again, close to his chest, kissing me with biting teeth. He tangles a fist in my hair and pulls my head to one side with gentle force, exposing my sensitive neck. For a moment I have the bizarre sense that I'm about to be bitten, infected with some kind of vampiric poison. And I don't fear a thing. I want whatever Adrian has in store for me, without question. Without doubt. I trust him implicitly, and I long for him to mark me.

"I can't seem to keep my hands off of you," Adrian growls, his voice low and rasping at my ear, sending a shiver down my spine. His lips hover just behind the shell of my ear, his breath warm and ticklish on my neck. Then he dives forward and kisses me there, his lips sucking at my soft flesh until yet another mark begins to darken, added to the line of purplish-pink splotches he's already left behind. It's like a signature, like a tattoo on my skin, branding me as his own.

"I need you," I whisper, my eyes rolling back in my head. "I've always needed you, I just didn't know until we met. You've been in here, coursing through my veins for so long…"

Adrian moves me a little so he can position the head of his cock at my ready opening. With both his strong arms still supporting me completely in the chilly lake water, he lowers me down onto his cock, spearing me as I ride him. I cry out with delight as he pushes fully inside of me, filling me up so perfectly, like we are made for each other, two inter-locking puzzle pieces finally reunited.

I am amazed at his incredible strength and control. He bounces me up and down on his cock so easily, like I weigh nothing at all. Sure, the water makes me a little more buoyant, but my body is almost totally out of the water, lifted up with my legs wrapped tightly around Adrian's waist. He grips me by the slope of my midsection, his fingers digging into my hips in a way that is simultaneously painful and sensual. I crave the pain. I need the tension. Because it makes the final release that much more exhilarating when it comes.

And come it does. Fast. And hard.

Before long I'm shrieking his name, calling out, "Adrian! Oh god, Adrian!" as my body convulses with ecstasy. I feel so full, so complete, so overstimulated in the very best way. With every thrust I feel myself pushing closer and closer to another delicious edge. Adrian fucks me with abandon, lifting me up and slamming me down on his cock again and again.

"Fuck, Bex! You're so good, baby. Such a good girl," he groans in my ear, his breath coming fast and ragged by now. I can tell he wants to let go, he wants to give into the tidal waves of pleasure riding over him. I decide to help him along — he's always so in control, and I feel a sudden need to watch him lose it, totally give up. So I start to clench my pussy more tightly around his swollen cock, squeezing him as I bounce up and down. Adrian's hands grab at my shoulder blades for support, his mouth falling open as he lets out a groan of heady approval.

"Just like that, gorgeous, just like that," he murmurs roughly, leaning forward to kiss me as I ride him faster and faster. "Fuck, you're gonna make me come. Tell me you want it, baby girl."

"I want it," I moan between desperate kisses. "I want you to come, Adrian. Please."

"Tell me you're mine," he demands in a low growl. I tighten my cunt as much as I possibly can.

"I'm yours. I belong to you, Adrian," I whisper

breathlessly. I can feel Adrian's balls tightening up, his whole body tensing for the big release. "Please, I need you to give it to me," I go on, urging him to let go and fill me up like he's done before. I find myself hungry for his seed, greedy for it.

"Fuck, yes, baby!" Adrian groans through gritted teeth, and with one final thrust he pulls me closer to him and comes. Even with the cool water lapping up around my thighs and pussy lips, I can still feel his stream shooting up inside of me, filling me up so completely. I give a satisfied moan and collapse in his arms, feeling his cock spasm violently inside my cunt with the last few spurts of seed.

After a minute or so of standing huddled together like this in the lake, we finally let go, both of us laughing with exhilaration. Every single time we fuck, it feels like a new experience, like we redis-cover each other entirely with each kiss and touch. I've never felt this way before, so enraptured in Adrian's body, his words, his own pleasure. I want him to feel just as good as he makes me feel, and I know Adrian has the same desire for me.

We spend the next ten minutes or so just swim-ming around in the shallow waters, playfully splashing each other, laughing and joking. The sun is beginning to slip over the horizon, the forest surrounding us coming slowly to life. I can hear owls hooting, crickets chirping. The very moon above hangs heavy and luminous, like it's illuminated more brilliantly than usual just for our sakes.

"We should probably head out, huh?" I suggest, swimming up to Adrian and kissing him on the cheek. He grabs my face and kisses me full on the mouth, causing me to shriek and giggle.

"Yes. I have a feeling that swimming in the lake at night is just asking for trouble," he answers with a wink. "Besides, we still have a long way to go, don't we?"

I nod and take his hand, the two of us wading back to shore. We lean against the rental SUV for about five minutes, letting our bodies air dry slightly before patting ourselves down with a blanket from the backseat, getting dressed, and getting back on the road again.

As we drive down the curving, wild roads, I begin to hear another noise emerging from the soundtrack of nocturnal nature sounds and the low rumble of the SUV's engine. I furrow my brow, trying to determine whether it's thunder or… something else.

"Do you hear that?" I ask, turning to look at Adrian. To my dismay, there is a look of distinct concern on his face, which indicates to me that it probably isn't just thunder I'm hearing. "Adrian, what is it? What is that noise?"

"It sounds like motorcycles revving their engines," he replies flatly. I listen closely and realize that he's right; that's exactly what it sounds like. But there's not usually anyone else out here this time of night. It's a very sparsely populated area, and I don't recall ever seeing a motorbike on these roads.

The look on Adrian's face is enough to make my skin prickle with goosebumps. If my strong, courageous warrior is concerned... well, that doesn't bode well for me.

Motorcycle gangs tearing through rural areas aren't *that* uncommon, I tell myself, but I'd also be dishonest with myself if I ignored the memory of that silver-haired Russian back in the city. His eyes are still bright and piercing in my mind, and my instincts tell me he was looking at me with purpose.

But I try to dismiss it as we make our way further through the woods that are flitting by us, dense trees and brush getting thicker as we move deeper in. I know a lot of veterans who get back from their tours and feel jumpy for the next few *years* after they return. They have trouble sleeping because of what haunts their dreams, they act differently towards loved ones because of what happened in combat, and they find themselves without the support they need.

Nobody wants to go through that, and we fight

against it with every fiber of our being, but nobody who goes through it has a choice in the matter.

As I feel the SUV's rumble under me, I think back to the man, trying to search my memories for his face. I know how to memorize a face quickly, but the Russian I saw back in town doesn't ring any bells. Someone like that would stick out in my memory. In any case, he looks too old to be anyone I might have run into in my service days.

At least, that's my impression. But between the fireworks and my concern over what might be pursuing us, I'm not sure if I can even trust my own impressions.

I know Becca must be nervous. It takes a lot for someone like me to be put on edge, but then again, I have my PTSD episode looming over my shoulder, and despite everything good that's been happening lately, I feel it in my side like a knife, threatening to press in. It infuriates me, but I have to live with it.

Then I feel Becca lay one of her gentle hands on my massive one, and I'm able to control my reflexes and even feel some measure of comfort from the gesture. I look over at her and give a reassuring smile in return. She knows what I'm going through. This fight against myself would be twice as hard if I didn't have her at my side, regardless of all the mental and physical fortitude I've built up over the years.

I glance in her lap at her phone and notice it's

open to a radio streaming app, but it's just spinning its wheels. I wonder if she's trying to find that song once more. We must be too far in the country for a decent wireless signal to cut through the trees.

She closes out of the app in defeat and opens her mouth to speak. I'm expecting her to ask me if it's okay, if I'm feeling pain, or if I'm worried, but she never ceases to surprise me.

"Hey, no matter what, we're in this together."

I feel a smile come across my features as her words soothe me like a balm, and I turn my hand over to give hers a firm, comforting squeeze.

I see a hill up ahead, and I know that's the place to be. It's a good vantage point for what's coming.

"I'm going to pull over up here," I say in response, nodding over to the side of the road as I start to bring the vehicle to a stop.

"Why?"

"Need to make a call to a few friends," I explain, putting the car in park and climbing out of the seat. Being on the hill will help boost the cellphone signal, so hopefully I'll be able to get through.

There's something about the open road when you're stationary that makes you feel so far from everything else in the world. The gravel crunches beneath my feet as I step out of the car in the middle of the woods. It feels like emerging onto a giant's causeway, remote and derelict, save for the rumble of motorcycles in the distance. As comforting as the remoteness feels, to some degree, I can sense the tension in the air as thickly as I might sense the humidity of an incoming storm.

No, I tell myself, giving my head a shake as I pull out my phone, *I'm just being paranoid. You're back in a stable part of the world, Adrian, you don't need to see shadows in every corner.* I might not need to, but I do. And I can't help but remind myself that the last time I dealt with shadows in every corner, a good man died.

I want to call one of my old squad mates up. I've wracked my memory over and over for a clue about that silver-haired guy, but maybe one of my men has better recall than I do. But when I put my phone to my ear, I hear a flat tone, and I glance at the screen to realize that I have no service.

I have an impulse to mutter a curse, but I don't want to do anything else to put Becca more on edge. I satisfy my urge by squeezing the phone until I feel something start to give, then stick it back into my pocket.

"No service," I call to the car, and I see Becca's anxious face nod, glancing behind us. I've noticed it too: the rumble of the motorcycles is getting louder by the second.

"It's still at least a half-hour to my parents' house," Becca says as I climb back in the car, "but this road isn't patrolled very much."

"Good," I say, putting the key into the ignition,

"I'm not too keen on meeting whoever's rolling up behind us."

"What's been bothering you about it, Adrian?" she asks, putting her hand on my arm again, furrowing her brows. "Canada isn't exactly known for its fierce biker gangs."

"Exactly," I say in a low tone, turning the key.

The ignition clicks.

I can practically feel the color draining from Becca's face, but equipment malfunction is something I've had to deal with on a daily basis in the military. I try a couple more times to start the ignition, getting the same dull click.

"Battery's dead," I say, finality in my voice as I turn around and reach into the backseat, rummaging around in my bag.

"Dead?" she says, the edge of alarm in her voice. "We don't have a cell signal out here, Adrian, what do we—"

"Get ready," I answer before she can finish, drawing my pistol out from my bag in the back seat, loading a round in the chamber and glancing into the rear-view mirror.

I hear Becca take in a sharp breath, looking at me in confusion a moment before blinking a few times as she realizes the sounds of the motorcycle engines are getting closer. "How did you get that into the country?!"

"It's not the first time I've had to smuggle

weapons in," I say calmly. That's the simplest part of everything going on right now, truthfully. "That, and a few friends on the inside. Never know when you'll be stranded in the woods with a gang on your tail."

"Are you sure about this, Adrian?" she asks, trying desperately to keep her voice even. I glance over at her. I know this must be a lot to process in such a short time. She left behind everything to do with high-adrenaline firefights and firearms years ago. As far as I know, she might even be suspecting that I'm being triggered into another episode. And truthfully, I feel like I'm slipping back into my natural role, but she must feel like she's slipping back into a nightmare.

It's a feeling I can understand well. So it's up to me to guide her through that nightmare however I'm able.

"I know you think I'm being overly cautious, Becca," I say, reaching out to stroke her hair, showing her just how steady my hands are in the face of uncertainty in the wilderness. "And that's not an instinct you should lose. But experience has punished me for not being prepared for the totally unexpected. If I'm thinking too far into this, then these bikers will, in all likelihood, pull over and offer us a hand to the nearest mechanic."

I glance into the mirror again. The bikes are going to be on us any second now.

"But if I'm right, and I'm not ready, then the

consequences will be worse. So I need you to trust me, Bex," I say, taking her hand and kissing it as I look deeply into those eyes, a storm of emotion within them. "Get into the back seat and lay down on the floor. Don't move from there until I tell you it's safe, do you understand?"

Without a moment's hesitation, Becca nods. She doesn't smile — she knows that niceties need to wait for now. She hauls herself over the middle console and gets down onto the floorboards. As she does, I start rolling down the driver's side window. She hears the sound and raises her head a moment.

"What's that for?"

"Just trust me," I say calmly, and she complies, lowering herself as much as possible. I hear her take a deep breath, just as I'm taking one at the sight of the bikers appearing over the horizon behind us.

It only takes one glance at the gleaming black weapons in their hands for my combat training to kick in.

I dive for the passenger's seat and kick the door open just as the sounds of bullets ring out across the forest.

The gunmen take the bait, and as I move back to the driver's seat, bullets riddle the interior of the door where they thought someone was about to burst out. As their attention is focused on the passenger's side, I use the driver's side door to rest my shooting arm on and take aim in the side mirror.

I assess them in less than a fraction of a second. There are four of them. The three firing at the door are wielding Uzis, unleashing a spray of bullets in the general vicinity of wherever they point. If they kill anyone with those out here, it would be sheer luck. They intended to scare their victims out of the vehicle.

I'm not half so foolish.

The man in the front of the pack, though, holds a military-grade Kalashnikov shotgun in his hand, and by the look of him, he's someone of authority.

But one thing stands out to me above all the rest in this crew of assassins: none of them are wearing the colorful yet highly specific patches that would betray them as members of a biker gang. These kinds of gangs pride themselves in their work. If it were some crew of bangers out for glory, they'd be flying their colors. These men are after something different altogether.

In that split second, the leader is the only one who notices my pistol out. He veers out of the way just as I line him up in my sights, but I'm not about to let the shot go. I fire off a quick, precise round, and one of the Uzi gunmen's brains spray out behind him in a fine mist before the weight of his body lays down the bike and sends it skidding across the road.

His comrades have to swerve to avoid him, and I hear shouts of expletives in Russian. Glass shatters in the back window as I lower myself down, the bullets hitting all around me and piercing the front windshield as well.

But I take advantage of the confusion on the road. As the men swerve, I line up a shot at just the right trajectory ahead of the nearest one while he's distracted, and I fire off another round that catches him at the base of the skull, killing him instantly.

He falls off his bike to his left, and the vehicle skids out from under him and screeches toward the front of our car.

I have a window of opportunity.

The leader has already whipped around, and he's aiming a shot at the front of the car as his bike carries him forward like a torpedo.

I could hold my position and get down low, but I realize that would send the bullets on a path right for Becca. I can't allow that. Even if it means risking exposing myself.

So within a split second of his arrival, I dive out of the car and for the cover of the fallen motorcycle. I hear a loud blast, and the shotgun peppers both the motorcycle and the front of the car with bullets that would have killed me instantly.

I waste no time in standing up from cover the next moment and firing a round into the leader's head, precise as a machine, before he can do so much as see if his shot touched me. But I'm unscathed, and he topples off his bike and sprawls down into the ditch beside the road. Food for the buzzards circling overhead already.

The last man riding looks over his shoulder, seeing his comrades dead on the ground, me standing over the ruins without so much as a scratch on me. I see his mouth move as he forms an expletive, and rather than turning to try to avenge his fallen brothers, he puts the pedal to the metal and tries to blaze down the road, weaving back and forth to evade a shot.

Coward.

I'm not ready to let him escape so easily. Even if I could afford to let him report to his superiors, I have no sympathy for craven wretches who'd leave their comrades to rot out in the country sun.

I drop to one knee, taking my time as I breathe deeply, watching the pattern of his weaving for a few moments. As easily as anyone else might sign their name, I hold my breath, line up the shot ahead of where he'll be, and fire the round.

A moment later he wobbles, flails, then he hits the ground after a bullet sails through his spine, and his bike rolls on top of him, crushing him under the hot metal.

The silence that follows is deafening. My heart rate slows down, and I tell myself that all of them are indeed down as I glance back to the SUV. My first thought is of Becca.

I sprint towards the vehicle, nearly ripping the

back door open to see her terrified face looking up at me, unharmed.

Relief washes over both our expressions at the same time as I pull her out and hug her tight into me, feeling her let out a sob as I squeeze her.

"It's okay, baby," I whisper into her ear. "It's over. They're finished. Are you hurt?"

"Are *you*?" she gasps, looking up at me and putting her hands on my strong jaw. I grin.

"Me? I can take a bullet or five. But no, I'm fine."

Her lip quivers, but she breaks down into a mix of crying and laughing as I hug her again, stroking her back reassuringly. But then she looks back at the SUV and nearly collapses in shock, looking at the devastated vehicle.

"It's...it's ruined," she breathes. "We're stranded!"

"The car was dead anyway," I say grimly. "Not much use to us now."

"Who were they?" she asks, looking over at the carnage all around us. I can see her eyes drifting to their leather jackets as well, her brow furrowing. "They... don't look like a biker gang."

I stride over to the body of the leader, and she follows at my heels. I turn his body over and look into his vacant, dead eyes before I pop his jacket open, then start ripping his shirt in two to confirm my suspicions.

"These men don't wear patches," I say in a low tone before pulling the ripped shirt back to reveal his bare chest. "They wear something more permanent."

Becca's eyes widen as she looks at the body. Emblazoned across the man's chest is a large, red, eight-pointed star. The emblem of the Russian mafia.

I'm sitting in the backseat of Adrian's bullet-riddled rental SUV, poring over the contents of my purse, in a dazed state of confusion and mild panic. I keep reminding myself that I have seen worse. I have witnessed terrible things, and this should not affect me so strongly. I have seen death. I have heard gunshots and the sickening crunch of fallen bodies on the unforgiving earth. But still... something has definitely changed — I have definitely changed — and I can't just compartmentalize as well as I used to.

I know exactly what the difference is, why I can't seem to put all this fear aside. My gut is twisting with anxiety and nausea, my thoughts muddled and frenzied as my poor brain tries to make sense of what's just happened. I know this place so well. This rural road holds sweet memories for me, learning how to ride a bike, playing hide and seek with my cousins when I was a child. The forest is so thick and overgrown that there are endless places to hide when you're very small. And of course, having grown up here, I was never very afraid of getting lost.

But now there are streaks of blood marring the otherwise pristine pathway. There are circular, serpentine marks on the ground from where the motorcycles swerved and revved their engines. And still, none of this would have too strongly affected the Rebecca Summers of a few years ago. Back when I was totally in control of my own emotions and actions — well, with the exception of how I felt about Adrian — and it took a hefty heap of trauma to knock me off-kilter. But nowadays, I'm not so unshakable, and it's easy to figure out why.

Now I'm a mother.

This world is not just my own to navigate, I now have to contend with the fact that such horrors and tragedies coexist alongside the innocent, guileless little girl I gave life to. Maya's sweet, smiling face is ever-present in the forefront of my mind, and it's difficult to balance out the contrast of such childlike goodness with the bloody smears of death on the road which always led me home.

It's hard to come to terms with the fact that a world which can bring forth such terrible suffering and fear can also create angelic young souls like

Maya. I want to protect her, especially since my work with NATO armed forces gave me a glimpse into the darkest shadows of the human condition. I know just how bad it can get out here, which is why I am so fiercely protective of my little girl. That's why the very same day I found out for certain that I was pregnant, I immediately began to see the world differently. Suddenly, every close call, every adjacent danger that I might have shrugged off in the past, all at once became too real, too close for comfort. Because I knew that I was no longer simply guarding my own life, which is mine to either guard or wager as I please, but the life of my unborn child, innocent of all this.

So I left service, leaving my dangerous back-ground totally behind. Suddenly my mission to save the world seemed... well, silly. I realized that while I couldn't save the whole world by myself, I could certainly save my daughter as much pain as possible. Once I left NATO and returned to my former quiet, slow-paced life in Canada, I never really looked back. It almost feels now like that was somebody else's life, or some film I watched. It's hard to believe that the woman who treated bullet wounds and listened to horror stories of native people losing their young children to insurgents and even to American soldiers... is me. I am simply not the same person anymore, and I owe it all to Maya.

Still, some part of my NATO training remains,

having lain dormant for years. But now I'm remembering my skills, my obedience and sense of discipline, because I am being thrust back into a sort of battle front. If there is one thing that has stayed with me the most, it's my ability to fall in rank. And out here, out of my element and out of practice, Adrian becomes my commanding officer with ease. He is a natural leader, and while I consider myself to be a leader, too, I know that this is not a battle I was made to fight. It's been years since I last had to contend with real death and fear like this, so I know it's better to listen to Adrian on this. He's more recently returned from war. This is still his element, even though it breaks my heart to think that way.

So when he told me to leave my purse behind but remove anything that might bear my address or any of my parents' information, I immediately start to do as I'm told. And as I look over all the various contents of my bag, I bite my lip, feeling a rush of fear and sadness come over me.

There are the usual suspects, like lipstick, tissues, keys, my cell phone which is totally dead, a pack of gum, and a little notepad and pen. And then there are the accoutrements of life as a single mother. There's an old pacifier of Maya's, the crumpled up scribble she made one day in the car when she got ahold of a restaurant receipt and a crayon, and a business card given to me by her pediatrician, informing me of when her next checkup appointment is. My eyes start to sting with tears and I bite the inside of my cheek to keep from crying. I used to be so strong. Nothing could hurt me. But now... I just miss my daughter. And I fear for her.

"Adrian, what if — what if they find my family?" I ask softly, my voice trembling despite my best efforts to keep it even and calm. He's been walking around the area, his eyes hawk-like and his expression stern. He's going straight back into wartime mode, and while it's definitely appreciated, it also just reminds me of darker times that I have tried so hard to leave behind me in the past.

Adrian stops and looks over at me from across the road where he's been surveying the dead man's chest tattoo. The sharpness in his gaze softens when he locks eyes with me.

"I won't let them harm your family — our family," he assures me, and I know he must be thinking of Maya, too. He hasn't met her, but with the millions of pictures I showed him, at least now he has a face to put to the name. That undoubtedly makes her more real, more present in his thoughts. Which would normally warm my soul and give me butter-flies in my stomach, but right now all I can think about is how afraid I am — for Maya, for Adrian and me.

"I'm scared," I confess. "I have worked so hard to put my past behind me, for Maya's sake. I can't stop thinking about what might happen if they find her… what they might do to her…"

Adrian closes the distance between us in several quick, long strides, bending down to kiss my forehead while he cups my cheeks with both hands. "Becca, I promise you nothing is going to happen to your family. I will do whatever it takes to keep them safe. Especially our daughter."

"I feel so out of place now," I tell him softly. "This isn't my element anymore. I-I'm not a warrior like you are, Adrian. I'm just a mom now, and I'm so afraid. I want to protect her but I don't know how. I don't understand what's going on here. Who are these guys and what do they want with us?"

Adrian sighs heavily, and I can tell he's holding something back.

"These Russians… they're not after you. They're after me. But now that they've seen us together, they'll know I have a new weak spot, a new vulnerability. Which is why we have to make sure they have no way of tracking you or your family down. It's an advantage that your folks live so far out in the country. These guys don't know this area like you do. But we have to throw them off as much as we can."

"Is that why I'm supposed to leave my purse behind?" I ask.

Adrian nods. "Yes. Don't leave anything that could tip them off to who you are and where you live. The less they know about you and your life, the less likely they can harm you. But leaving the purse makes it look like they might have captured you. So that when the next round of cavalry comes by and sees the SUV broken down here, they might not expect that you got away safe."

"But what about the bodies in the road?" I press on, swallowing hard as I force myself not to look around at the scene of destruction laid out around us.

"Let me take care of that," he replies gravely. "I'm going to hide them off the road. Just wait here and keep looking to make sure there's nothing left in your purse that could identify you or your family. You want to be totally certain."

"Then what?" I question, terrified of the answer.

"We'll have to move on. We have our duffel bags. I have rations. I have weapons. And you're more familiar with these woods than I am. It's getting closer to midnight and we can't go far in the dark, but we'll at least get a start before making camp for the night," he explains. My blood runs cold at the thought of tromping through the dense forest with Adrian in the dark. Although these woods are pretty much my home, it's been a long time since I ventured away from the beaten path, and I get the sense that we aren't going to be able to stay near the road. It's too dangerous.

Still, I can't exactly come up with a better plan than what Adrian's proposing, so I simply return to dutifully cleaning out my purse. I take my driver's license, credit cards, and notepad — the latter has my name emblazoned across the front – and leave just about everything else. Except for the items which indicate that I have a child. With a heavy heart, I decide to do my own little burial ceremony, only instead of laying to rest the bodies of murderous Russian motorcyclists, I'm tucking away the pacifier, pediatrician's card, and Maya's little crayon scribble.

I take about twenty steps off the road into the woods and dig a little hole with a broad piece of broken branch, then drop these items in and cover them back up with dirt. This way, even if I lose my duffel bag or, even worse, I am captured by the enemy, at least I won't have any mementoes tipping them off to the existence of my daughter.

Then I walk back to the dead SUV and wait for Adrian to return from his own burial process. He comes back about twenty minutes later, looking very disheveled, his nice clothing stained with dirt.

"Are they... are they totally covered up?" I ask nervously. Adrian nods and puts an arm around me, helping me out of the backseat.

"Yeah. They're buried under dirt and branches. It's a shallow grave, but at least it means they're off the road. What about you; are you all packed and ready to go?" he asks.

"I guess so," I reply, and I suppose the sadness in

my voice is more evident than I intended for it to be, because Adrian gives me a regretful, heartbreaking look. He pulls me into a tight embrace, stroking my hair.

"I know it's hard to leave this behind," he says gently, his breath warm on the top of my head. His hands slide down my back and I melt into his arms, closing my eyes.

"I never wanted my daughter to be exposed to the kinds of things I saw over there in the desert, Adrian. I wanted to keep her safe from stuff like that," I admit, a tear rolling down my cheek. Back when I was with NATO, I prided myself on being able to stay rational and calm even under extreme pressure. It took a LOT of stress to make me crumple and fall apart, and even seeing blood and sickness and death and suffering day in and day out was usually not enough to make me cry.

But now... all I can think about is Maya. And about my newly rekindled love affair with her father, this beautiful and powerful man holding me close on the side of the wooded road. And I just feel like it's all slipping away through my fingers. For a moment I got a glorious glimpse of what could be, of the wonderful life I could have led, the perfect family I nearly had. I want that more than anything — to be free and happy and unafraid, for my daughter to grow up with that same joy and fearlessness.

The thought of losing that is more devastating than any horror I witnessed overseas.

"Don't cry," Adrian whispers, squeezing me close to him. "Everything is going to be okay, I swear to you. I will keep you safe. I will get us out of this. You just have to trust me. Do you?"

I push back slightly and look up into his face, the earnest expression in his vivid green eyes, and I nod my assent. "Yes. I'm terrified and I'm sad, but I trust you, Adrian."

"Then we'll be just fine. Stick close behind me, Bex. We've got to get moving if we're gonna get enough space between us and the road before it's time to make camp for the night," he says. We leave the scene of the carnage behind, the dead SUV parked lopsided on the side of the road as the two of us venture out into the unwelcoming woods.

The trees overhead are so thick and bushy that we can hardly make out the luminous orb of moonlight dangling somewhere above us, and the light from Adrian's pocket-sized flashlight is dim and limited at best. At first, he insisted on carrying both duffel bags, wanting to spare me any extra discomfort and pain, but I put my foot down and reassured him that I am as strong now as I ever was — in fact, maybe more so from years of carrying a baby and her supplies around. So he gives up my duffel bag and I hoist it over my shoulders, following him more deeply into the forest.

There are eerie sounds all around us as the woods awakens and comes to life. Owls and other nocturnal birds of prey cry out, their ominous calls echoing through the dark woods. I can hear the rustling of the underbrush from all angles, and there is the distinct high-pitched chatter of bats flying overhead now and again. These sounds are usually rather comforting to me when I'm sitting on the front porch of my parents' house in the evening, Maya babbling and getting sleepy on my lap, and a glass of red wine in my hand. But at the moment I don't feel particularly comforted by my surroundings. I have the strong sense that I am out of place, that I am somewhere I do not belong, and the chattering forest knows it, too.

Adrian and I trek for what seems like a couple miles before he stops us and announces that we've got to set up camp for the night. I have no idea where we are at this point, having gotten a little swept up in my own thoughts rather than paying much attention to the direction in which we were traveling. Although really, it would not have mattered much even if I had been paying close attention; these woods have changed a lot since the carefree days of my youth, and besides, it's too dark at night to navigate through even for an experienced hiker.

So Adrian unravels an oversized bed roll, which to my relief is more than large enough for both of us to cuddle into comfortably. Still, he insists on letting me sleep alone first, wanting to look over me while I rest. He smiles and does his best to banish my paranoia, but I can still tell that he is worried. And that realization makes it very, very difficult to fall asleep. They're out there... somewhere. Was that noise them?

As I watch Becca drift off into sleep, I take a deep, quiet breath, letting the sounds of the crickets and the low, crackling fire sink into the world around me.

I take a seat on a stump nearby, moving quietly despite the fact that we're a good ways into the woods. I've taken the necessary precautions, even if the men coming after us clearly aren't the sorts who know how to take on someone like me. No Spetsnaz operatives would have carried on the messily bungled operation like the one I took care of earlier.

Still, I find my eyes looking into every shadow of the woods around us, specters of the night conjured up in my mind's eye by the low light of the fire I've built. No smoke rises from my fire, thanks to the dry wood I was so picky about using for it.

Those road hogs aren't planning to look into the

woods, but there's a good chance they'll find the bodies of the men I killed, and when they do, they might well come after us.

If that happens, my pistol is at my side, along with a couple guns I took from the dead. I'm ready for them.

Becca's chest rises and falls softly as she lies on her back, her beautiful eyes closed gently as she faces the starry sky. She looks so serene there on the ground, even though I know she's not asleep yet. I've learned how to tell when someone's really asleep or not over the years. But it's been a hell of a day for her, so I know the exhaustion is going to get the better of her anxiety before very long.

Even so, seeing her form lying there on the ground, looking at those curvy hips that bore my child, the breasts I've ravaged and will ravage again soon, it all fills me with protective instincts unlike any I've ever known. It's something new and powerful I feel deep inside me. My hand grips the handle of my pistol as I tear my eyes from her, turning my ear to the distant sound of motorcycles.

It's at the thought of what I have to protect here at home that my mind wanders to the Russians back on the road that I slew, leaving them to rot in the wilderness.

There's no doubt in my mind now that I brought the war back home with me. There's such a cruel injustice to everything about this feud with the Russians.

They never should have been at the same site as us on that fateful night. They never should have stormed in with guns blazing on us, not knowing what we were doing there. There never should have been any deaths that night.

None of it should have ever happened, and worst of all, it never should have followed me back home.

What of the other men in my squad, I wonder? Are they being targeted for hits as well? Are they as prepared for danger as I've been? It's far more likely, though, that I'm the first target in the Russians' attempt at revenge. I'm the only one whose face they've seen, so I must have been the easiest for them to track. I wonder who was captured and tortured to divulge my name.

That aside, I was clearly the leader of that squad that took Russian pride. Killing me, the strongest among them, would send a message to the rest of the squad — it would strike fear into their hearts and scatter them. If the Russians went after my squad first, I would come after them before they could get far, and I'd be prepared.

And I think this Spetsnaz commander considered that in making his plans.

I watch one of the logs on the fire give way and crumble a bit, ember ashes floating up into the air far above us, looking like a few scattered fireflies around the campsite. I smile a little. It's funny, I could see myself taking Becca on a cute little camping trip in a nice, wooded area, just us and the stars and nothing else in the world.

But the sounds of motors in the distance remind me that there can be no peace. I'm a man on the run, and the Russians won't hesitate to either kill my Bex or steal her to be put to some terrible fate. The very thought makes my blood boil, and I almost wish the bastards *would* find us.

The more biker bodies I can leave for the buzzards on this godforsaken road, the stronger the message I can send back to the Russians.

I gaze down at Becca again and realize she has indeed fallen into a deep sleep, the rising and falling of her chest more automated, her hands relaxed at her sides, head turned. I could look on her all night, she's so peaceful, like an angel in repose.

As much as I love Becca, I know I'm at a disadvantage here because of her, on this playing field. When I was out doing missions for the service, I had nothing to lose. My team operated as one, all of us there voluntarily, all of us knowing the risks, and most importantly, all of us prepared to handle them.

Becca can handle herself decently in the field, but she's not equipped to deal with armed gangs of the Bratva, much less the Russian Special Forces operatives orchestrating the whole thing.

I have someone very, very dear to me at my side,

and thanks to that silver-haired biker back in town, everyone coming after us knows it.

My heart suddenly feels so heavy, and I look down at Becca with a hint of apology in my eyes.

She deserves so much better than this. Maya deserves so much better than this. Oh god, Maya — if the Russians did enough digging, I suspect it wouldn't be hard for them to find her. I haven't been as honest as I could with Becca about just how precarious of a situation we're in. I can't give her that mental burden.

She already has so much to deal with.

I run my fingers through my hair, glancing out among the trees and shadows as the weight of it all presses down on me.

I never should have come back into Becca's life. I might not have known the Russians would come after me, but as long as the mere risk was there, I should have kept my distance. Tied up loose ends. Contacted an embassy, even conduct a more violent cleanup of the witnesses to what happened, anything to protect my new family back home.

I feel so blindsided by it all, though. I didn't know I had a family to protect, just a selfish urge to go and meet up with Becca again. I didn't know someone was out for revenge. All rookie mistakes. How could I let myself screw up this badly in such a short time?

I clench my jaw, remembering words of wisdom that were passed down to me what feels like a lifetime ago. The crackling firelight in front of me takes me back into my memories, to the first time there was a casualty in a squad I served with.

I'm a rookie again, fresh into the SEAL service. Instead of the fire that warms me and Becca, I'm staring into the burning remains of the ramshackle pirate compound on the hot Somalian shore, its embers providing the only remaining light in the moonless night's sky. It should have been a flawless operation — in and out, wipe the remains of the human trafficking ring off the map, and extract the victims unharmed. All of that has been accomplished, and the rest of the men are loading the half-starved prisoners onto our boat while I stand over the body of one of my comrades. He was caught by a pirate sniper we hadn't anticipated — Intel told us they didn't have long-range weaponry, so they must have gotten the rifle that very day. I feel my commander put a hand on my shoulder, and I meet his steady gaze as I clench my fist around my friend's dog tags.

"O'Connor," he addressed me, "I want you to listen close, because you're going to lead a squad one day, and you're going to need to say this to your own men. All this intel, all the planning that goes into these operations that make it seem more air-tight than brain surgery?" He shakes his head. "It's a house of cards, O'Connor. We're not making plans in a vacuum or the war games. We're trying to stay afloat in the ocean in a typhoon. Just because we're better at swimming than most other people doesn't mean we're all going to make it to shore. And if

you blame yourself every time a rogue wave takes someone underwater..." He crouches down, picking up the body of a man I trained next to for years. "Then you may as well jump right in with them."

Those words stuck with me, like some kind of fucking ghost that prodded me in the back at the same time that it kept me grounded. I wanted to prove him wrong so damn much that I nearly quit the service out of frustration. But he proved right over the years.

And after extraction that night in Syria, I found myself passing the same words along to the rest of my squad.

Becca turns in her sleep, rolling onto her side, her voluptuous figure a warming comfort to me in the still night. In that moment, I know what I have to do.

In a silent prayer, I vow that I will do whatever it takes to protect Becca in the storm I've brought home with me. I can't save everyone, and I'd go mad if I tried, but I'm going to save Becca and Maya or die trying.

Unfortunately for the Russians, I don't die easily.

Part of me wants to rein myself in, remind myself that I'm going to be a civilian now. There are instincts honed to perfection in my body that I fight tooth and nail every morning to suppress. I'm a hunter of men, a cold and calculating killer. I've brought down warlords and politicians alike without breaking a sweat. I told myself that I would put that part of myself into the grave before I came home and brought Becca into my life.

But I have a family now. That part of me I tried so desperately to hide might be my only chance of getting us out of this mess alive.

My mind flits back to the half-serious thought of tracking down the men responsible for this, and I realize that's exactly what I'm going to have to do.

Old instincts come back to me flawlessly, though, as I begin thinking through the situation like a mission.

It's not uncommon for Russian military to fall in with the Bratva, the Russian mafia, after leaving the service. Like so many American veterans who end up on the street or in worse condition, the Russians often leave the service to find themselves without a support network for their mental and physical health, finding their friends and family to have moved on with life.

Such people have many reasons to find life in the Bratva attractive. Like military service, they have their strict hierarchies, their tight bonds between comrades, and their singular ruthlessness. And the money is good.

The Russian mafia in America has a very strong presence, and their resources and pockets can run very, very deep. Former Spetsnaz operatives would find the Bratva welcoming their killing and tracking skills with wide open arms and wallets. It's likely that this vengeful Russian is someone who's risen through the ranks in a very short amount of time.

This is both an advantage and disadvantage for me. Such a man has a lot of blood on his hands, no doubt, and many of his promotions probably came out of fear as much as respect. Many of his underlings, like these bikers, will jump at his command, and it may be hard to convince any of them to divulge clues as to his identity or whereabouts.

But men who rocket through the ranks make many enemies, too. There may well be rivals waiting for my Spetsnaz friend to slip up so they can strike him down a few pegs. Better yet, he may even have an over boss of some kind getting nervous about him. Killers of the mob who become very powerful and very deadly tend to make their superiors nervous, with good reason.

The question now, then, is whether I can learn enough about my enemies to start wedging in divisions between them.

Of course, the easiest solution would be to simply round up as many of them as I can and wipe them from the face of the earth. But that kind of planning takes time we simply don't have.

But I'm getting ahead of myself. First things first: we'll get an early start in the morning and make for the nearest town, where I can get some cell reception. From there, I can start gathering information and putting out feelers for old contacts that will get me what I need to exact justice on these men.

From then, it's just a matter of time before I can start hunting down these killers like the dogs they are. As the thought crosses my mind, it strikes me how little sympathy I have for these men, how readily I'm able to devise plans to end their lives.

Many of them have families, too. A few might even have kids of their own. I wonder what kind of life the Russian operative out for my blood had? What did he leave behind when he started coming after me? The men I killed in Syria had hopes and dreams, too, but I killed them all the same. How many lives did I ruin? What kinds of friendships did my actions end bloodily?

Yet none of those thoughts deter me from what I know in my heart I have to do. No matter how relentless the Russians are, no matter what they're fighting for, the most important woman in the world to me is sleeping at my feet. She carried our child and brought her into this world. She gave me hope and passion to hold onto while I was out in the field. For all I know, I just put another baby into her womb, and the thought of that makes my cock grow, wanting to keep her pregnant as much as her heart desires. And I'm going to do whatever it takes to protect her.

But that thought gives me pause, too. I clench my fist, the hand that's taken lives before and will take lives again. If I want to go through with this plan, I have to become the ruthless killing machine I was while I served the SEALs. And there's a thought haunting me, nagging at the back of my mind as I walk myself through every potential means of assassinating the enemies.

Will Becca still love the monster I must become?

I'm running through the forest in the dark, my long white dress ripped and stained from the branches and vegetation reaching out toward me as I pass. My eyes dart frantically back and forth, scanning the overgrown path in front of me, and my feet pound the cool earth with every frenzied step. I have to move faster, I have to keep going, even though my chest is growing tight and my lungs are gasping for oxygen. My own heart beat is rushing loudly in my ears and I'm scared that my legs might give out beneath me, but I have to go on. There is an ominous alarm going off in my head, telling me that the forces I'm running from are just behind me, hot on my trail, and if I slow down or falter for even a brief moment, they will catch up to me and that will be the end of it.

Somewhere toward the horizon, waiting for me, is my parents' home. An escape from this terrible chase, where I can hide away and wait for the troubles to simply pass me by. I know that if I just keep going I will eventually make my way to safety, but I keep tripping over the hem of my ankle-length dress, so I clutch at the fabric of my skirt with both hands, tearing through the woods like a runaway ghost in white.

What am I running from?

I almost cannot dare to ask the question, because I am terrified of the answer.

What lies behind me that could instill such fear in me? What could possibly be lurking in my past which could make me feel so panicked?

Suddenly, the trees melt away on all sides, thinning out until I can see the sky above in front of me — only it's no longer nighttime, and the moon has been replaced by an oppressively hot, blinding golden sun. I look around in confusion to find that the forest is gone, and I am surrounded by miles and miles of sand. I'm running through the desert dunes and I have no idea where I'm going.

"Take me back!" I try to scream, pleading with what-ever supernatural force has picked me up and deposited me so far from home. I was almost there — I was almost safe! And now I don't have any idea how to get back. And my voice is totally gone. No matter how hard I try to yell, not a single breath of sound comes out of my mouth. What is happening to me?

I stumble to the sandy ground, curling up into a little ball and trying to shield myself from the horrors that are undoubtedly right behind me, poised to pounce upon me and rip me apart. With my heart hammering away in my chest, I turn to face my attacker, readying myself for the end.

But as soon as I turn around, there is a deep, rumbling, earth-shattering voice calling my name, distracting me from my current panic. "Becca," the voice growls, seeming to come from the very sky.

"Wake up," says the male voice, and I do as I'm told — instantly.

I sit straight up and let out a breathless little yelp as my eyes open and I start to look around, totally confused and disoriented. I'm not in a bed, and I'm not even inside a hotel room. On all sides I am surrounded by the deep, dark woods, and I don't remember at first how I even got here. But then Adrian's calming, deep voice reassures me, "It's okay. You were having a bad dream."

I feel his massive hand on my shoulder, steadying me and comforting me. Bringing me back to the present moment. I turn and look toward him, blinking blearily in the dim light of dawn. He is crouching beside me, wearing an expression of concern. It all rushes back to me in that moment — our passionate reunion, our whirlwind days of traveling together toward home, and then the violent scene with the motorcycle gang. That's why I'm in the woods and I feel so nervous.

"I-I'm sorry," I murmur, raking a hand back through my hair and sighing heavily. "I don't usually have nightmares. In fact, I normally sleep like a baby. After having Maya, I learned to sleep through a lot of noise."

"Well, under the circumstances, I would say it's not a huge surprise," he answers, reaching down to stroke my cheek and give me a sympathetic smile. "Either way, you have nothing to apologize for. I drifted in and out for a few hours myself, and I can tell you that it was not the most peaceful slumber I've ever had."

"You could have asked me to take a shift," I tell him, feeling guilty for sleeping while he spent the majority of the night keeping watch over our little makeshift camp. He shrugs.

"Don't worry about it. I am the reason we're in this mess. Besides, I could hardly sleep knowing that you are vulnerable out here. It feels much more restful to watch over you than to go to sleep out here," he assures me, walking over to start packing things up and stamping out the campfire.

"What time is it?" I ask, then realize how silly a question that is. Neither of us have any way of telling the time — our phones are dead and we're in the middle of the wilderness.

But to my surprise, Adrian just glances up at the sky, his eyes calculating the angle of the sun's position in the clouds, then says, "Probably about six-thirty. Sorry to wake you so early, but it doesn't seem like that nightmare was doing you much good anyway."

I reach into my duffel bag lying nearby and pull out a stretchy black hair tie, then sweep my hair back into a messy, high ponytail. I know I must look a mess, but at least with my hair out of my face I feel a lot more put together and comfortable. Especially since today is likely to be long and arduous.

"So, are we still heading toward my parents' house?" I ask, brushing the tiny fragments of leaves off of my shirt. Adrian gives me a somewhat pained expression, his jaw tightening. Uh oh.

"Actually," he begins slowly, "I think it might be best if we stay away from your family for the time being, Bex. I hate to say it, but I don't want to risk being tailed by more of those Russians and have them follow us to your parents' home."

"Oh," I say, my stomach churning with anxiety. I can feel my heart sinking in my chest. I was so eager to go home and see my family, check on my baby girl. My parents have got to be so worried by now, since I haven't called in a few days and they knew I was due home the day before yesterday. I can't imagine how confused and scared Maya must be, missing her mother all this time. It was bad enough having to be away from her for a week while I was working for Mr. Green, but now the thought of being apart from my daughter even longer is almost more than I can bear. I miss her terribly, like a piece of my soul is gone when we're not together.

Adrian stops packing up and rolling the bed pack to walk over and take me by the hands, lifting them both up to his lips to kiss. His piercing green eyes are steadily trained on my face.

"I'm sorry, Bex," he says softly. "I never wanted to drag you back down with me. This isn't your battle to fight, and if I had known my past would follow me, I never would have brought them here to you. I understand if you resent me for ruining the peace and happiness you've found here."

Tears burn in my eyes at the prospect of Adrian thinking I would blame him for the trouble we're both in. It hurts to think that he assumes that. "Of course I don't blame you, Adrian. No matter what happens, I will never regret being reunited with you. I've missed you for so long — it's still surreal to see you standing here in front of me. And it's not your fault, any of this. You had no idea these guys would come after you. I don't blame you in the least. And we'll figure out how to deal with it together. You and me. I promise," I tell him firmly. And god, I hope I'm right.

Adrian smiles down at me and pulls me into a hug, stroking my hair. "You're just as strong and amazing as I remember," he says fondly. "I couldn't ask for anyone better by my side."

We finish packing up and start walking again,

following the sun in lieu of a clear pathway through the trees. This is pure wilderness, mostly untouched and totally intimidating, even for a girl who grew up around this area. The trees here are ancient, with gigantic trunks and far-reaching branches, casting enormous shadows on the ground below them. There is the constant background symphony of forest sounds — various bird calls, crickets and cicadas singing, the crunch of leaves and twigs underfoot, and the rustling of the brush all around us as small animals roam the forest unafraid of us. They are in their perfect element, but we are strangers here. For once, we are not the obvious top of the food chain. Out here, we are not superior animals — we are simply passers-through, and it is in our very best interest to be careful and respectful of the wildlife around us.

Even with the dangers of the woods lurking in the shadows, this place is undeniably beautiful, in a rugged, raw kind of way. It's amazing how gorgeous and awe-inspiring nature can be when it isn't muzzled and reined in by human intrusion. Adrian and I walk quietly for a couple miles, with me falling in rank behind him. My NATO armed-forces train-ing, which has lain long undisturbed and dormant, is now making its presence known again in the back of my mind. I remember how to follow orders, how to remain quiet and dutiful even under pressure. I force myself not to dwell too heavily on my painful thoughts of Maya and my parents, willing my mind to focus on the task at-hand. My senses are on fire, keen to the noises and smells and sights of the forest as I scan the scenery for potential dangers. I know Adrian is doing the same exact thing, his moss-green eyes narrowed as he watches out in front of us.

"I'm glad I decided to wear tennis shoes," I say aloud, more to myself than to Adrian.

"Me too," he replies, glancing back at me over his shoulder. "How are you feeling? I assume you probably haven't had to do much of this lately, since you left service a few years ago. If you need me to slow down or take a break, don't be afraid to speak up. I don't want to run you ragged."

"Oh, I'm fine," I assure him, waving my hand flippantly. And physically, that was true. In fact, even though I left my military position when I was pregnant with Maya, I continued to do strenuous exercises in order to maintain my shape and strength. One thing I loved most about my time with the armed forces was the feeling of pride I got when I looked in the mirror or engaged in high-stress, vigorous workouts. I loved being strong and powerful, and my sense of endurance has definitely aided me in my time as a single mother. Caring for an infant is much less stressful and physically demanding when you're used to arduous athletic training. So I have kept my body in tip-top shape, hoping that I would be able to be both a kickass mother and a kickass athlete in my own right.

"I've actually kept up a lot of my training," I tell him, a little proudly. Whereas most of the moms in my "new mommy" classes in the town closest to my parents' home complain of back-aches and sleepless nights, I have been lucky enough to claw my way through Maya's tempestuous first year relatively unscathed. I'm sure it helps that Maya herself has some fantastic genetics, courtesy of her unbelievably strong, handsome father. Even though she has my dark, silky hair, she inherited her father's beautiful green eyes and even his natural athleticism. She was sitting up on her own and crawling around a full two months before the baby books predicted she would.

"You know, our daughter is probably going to be one hell of an athlete," Adrian remarks, almost as though he can read my mind. "Between your graceful legs and my brute strength, I doubt we'll have to worry about having to fight off boys for her. She won't even need our help to defend herself, I bet," he adds, laughing. He looks back at me and I grin, nodding my agreement.

"That's true. And if she's anything like me, she'll do a great job of scaring them off with her awkwardness anyway. I wasn't exactly a boy-magnet growing up," I confess, rolling my eyes at the memory of being the only girl without a homecoming date, the only girl who dared to play sports with the boys.

"Awkward? No. I'm sure you just intimidated them with your beauty, brawn, and brains combination!" Adrian counters, slowing down to walk next to me instead of in front. I laugh and shake my head emphatically.

"Ohh no. Not the case at all. I was definitely not a popular girl in school," I tell him, shuddering as I think back to how much trouble I had with bullies growing up. "It was definitely a kind of me-against-the-world sort of thing. Kind of lonely, really."

Adrian gives me a sympathetic look, his eyebrows raised.

"That's a huge surprise," he admits. "I always assumed you just came out of the womb all sparkly and perfect."

"Oh, god no," I laugh, jabbing him gently with my elbow. "I was a loner. And a loser."

"Didn't you at least have a brother or sister to beat the bullies up for you?" he asks.

Sighing, I answer, "Nope. Only child."

"Damn, that does sound lonely," he says, shaking his head.

"What about you?" I pipe up, wanting to change the subject away from my pathetic adolescent struggles. "I'm one-hundred-percent certain you were a cool jock in school, right?"

He shrugs. "Well, yeah. Kind of."

"I knew it!" I giggle. "Let me guess, you were homecoming king?"

"Prom king, actually," Adrian corrects, with a wink.

"Oh my god. Of course you were," I groan, leaning into him. He puts an arm around my shoulder and pulls me in for a kiss.

"But you have to know that my school was very small. I grew up in a tiny little town in Idaho, Bex, and there weren't that many options to choose from for prom king. I just got lucky. I mean, hell, at least five percent of the student population was related to me. I had three brothers and two sisters," he tells me, and my jaw drops.

"Jeez! That's a huge family. I can't even imagine…" I trail off, in shock.

"Yep. And I was smack dab in the middle, too. Lots of competition. My three older brothers were all incredible athletes, and my little sisters were both musical geniuses. They won all kinds of choir awards and stuff. So naturally I had to do my very best to compete with all that," he explains, and I feel closer to him than ever. We've never discussed our childhoods or our pasts beyond our time together in the desert. We chat like this for hours, just walking through the woods and reminiscing, comparing our vastly different experiences growing up.

I have this warm, fuzzy feeling in my stomach as Adrian tells me all about his family, as it's clear he adores them all dearly. I can't wait for the day his family meets mine. It gives me a glowing sense of pride to think that my little girl has three uncles and two aunts she's never even met! Thinking about my family expanding so broadly is a welcome distraction from the situation at hand, and I find myself daydreaming about Maya growing up surrounded by all kinds of people who love her. Our daughter will be so deeply entrenched in love, and I just know that will shape her into a well-rounded, stable, compassionate person. That is all I want for her — to be loved and give love freely, without fear or hesitation.

Finally, we return to the topic of Maya's conception, and it turns out that we both have a confession to make. Adrian takes my hand and turns to me with wide, luminous eyes. Almost apologetic, but I don't know why until he starts explaining.

"Bex, I feel like I need to apologize for how rough I was with you the first night we slept together. I am usually more careful than that. More... gentle. I know I probably acted like an asshole, being so forceful with you," he says.

I shake my head and squeeze his hand, confused. To me, he hadn't come across as forceful, just powerful and passionate. "No, no. You weren't like that at all to me. I wanted it just as badly as you did. And it was nice to feel so wanted. Really."

He sighs, a burden clearly lifting from his broad

shoulders. "The truth is, shortly before we met up in that bar, I got the news that my mother had passed away," he confesses, hanging his head. "My mom was one of my best friends, even though we didn't always see eye to eye. She was my heart and soul, and for years she fought off the cancer. It kept going away and coming back, and she was a warrior through it all. But that day, the mail truck came through and I got the letter from my older brother telling me Mom had died. That's why I was in the bar. I was still trying to work through my grief, and you know what it's like… being a soldier. Everyone expects you to be strong. All the time. No matter what you're really feeling. So I did what every other heartbroken soldier did in the desert — I distracted myself with booze and sex."

"Oh my god," I gasp, totally taken aback. "I-I had no idea. I'm so sorry, Adrian."

He shakes his head. "No, I'm sorry. I let my emotions take over me. I was just so angry at myself for not being there for my mom in the end, when she needed me the most. I should have been home in Idaho. I should have been there for her. I know now that I wouldn't have been able to do anything to help her, but still. I felt responsible, in some twisted way, for her death. That's why I acted like such a callous womanizer when I was with you, Becca. I was griev-ing, and I didn't know how to deal with it. I'm sorry."

I lean forward and stand on tiptoes to kiss him

softly, reassuringly. "You have nothing to apologize for. I never once felt like you were taking advantage of me. I wanted you, too. And that night… well, it changed my life. For the better."

I pause for a moment, nervously considering whether or not to offer my own confession. But after he was so perfectly honest with me, I couldn't exactly justify hiding my own secret from him.

"Adrian, I have to admit something," I begin, looking up at him and biting my lip. He cocks his head to one side as though encouraging me to go on. "I-I… well, when I realized that the condom must have broken when we slept together… I was secretly overjoyed. That night with you was so magical, and I was so enraptured by you, that the thought of bearing your child sent me over the moon. Even if I never saw you again, I knew that any child of yours would be more than worth a lifetime of being a single mother. When I found out I was pregnant, it felt like I was carrying a piece of you with me, still, and that comforted me more than you could ever know."

Adrian beams down at me, then sweeps me into a passionate kiss. My entire body tingles at his insistent touch, and I feel myself melting into his arms, a willing victim.

"I know I have never met her, but I know that I love Maya already," he tells me softly, resting his forehead against mine. "I understand why you kept her secret from me at first. I wish you hadn't, but I can't hold it against you. You're a great mother for trying to look out for her, and I couldn't ask for a better partner in raising my little girl. I can't wait to meet her, and I promise the second we get through this mess, we'll be reunited and everything will be wonderful. As it should be."

"I know," I tell him quietly, resting my head on his chest. "I know."

"And soon we'll get to a town where we can use a phone to call some of my, uh, contacts to help us out. We're getting there, Bex. I swear," he adds, kissing the top of my head. Hand in hand, we continue walking, taking a break around noon to drink some water from a canteen in his duffel bag. To my relief, his soldier training has also taught him to never travel without some kind of sustenance on hand, so we eat some beef jerky and dried fruit for lunch.

We journey onward for a few more hours, and my feet are starting to ache by the time we stumble upon what looks like a partially-abandoned farm, just through a clearing. My heart flutters with antici-pation, thinking that we have finally found our oasis, our saving grace. We're free!

"Do you know who lives here?" Adrian asks in an undertone as we slowly approach the perimeter of the cleared land. I shake my head and shrug.

"No, but this land doesn't belong to my family anymore. It's privately owned, and I don't know the owners. I didn't even realize there was a farm out here," I admit, a little confused. The last I knew, our house was one of the few in this particular area. But then again, we've been walking in the opposite direction of my parents' home. So I don't think we are even in my usual stomping grounds anymore.

"I'll go to the main house and see if there's anyone home. Hopefully they will let us use their phone or at least point us in the direction of the nearest town center," Adrian tells me, urging me to stay behind just in case it isn't safe. I reluctantly agree, even though I think he might be acting a little over-cautiously. This is the country, and generally people are pretty friendly out here, even if they are a little standoffish at first. They just respect their own privacy, is all.

Just then, there is an air-splitting crack and a bullet comes hurtling over our heads, Adrian just barely ducking out of the way in time. He tackles me to the ground with a shout of "Get down!" and we both look around in frantic horror. What is going on?

Did someone really just fire a shot at us?!

*B*ecca shrieks, but my arm is already around her, and as if she were weightless, I haul her with me toward a large rock outcropping nearby, taking cover under it. Within moments, I've pushed her down into proper cover and draw my pistol.

I hear the sound of a shotgun reloading, but the click it makes tips me off to what must be going on, and I feel my muscles ease up just a hint.

Becca looks at me with utter fear in her eyes, terrified of what I suspected just a moment ago, but I reach over and put a large hand on her shoulder, giving it a reassuring squeeze and shaking my head.

A moment later, a voice from the shack confirms my suspicions.

"Damn police think you can come traipsing over my property without warning?" yells the scratchy voice of an older man, bearing the kind of hoarseness that comes from a voice that's not used very much. "I'm within my rights! I've got another couple rounds in this chamber, and I want to see a warrant or your backsides on your way back to the city, hear that? Damn suits!"

I have to suppress a laugh at the completely baffled look Becca gives me. "It's alright," I assure her, "out deep in the woods like this, every now and then you run into these guys who like to live off the grid. They're more than a little suspicious of outsiders, but they're usually not dangerous unless you sneak up on them or look like cops."

"And I'm guessing we're doing both?" she hisses back, and I give her a playful wink before turning my head and shouting back at the house's owner.

"We thought this place was abandoned!"

"Well, it's not!" he barks. "Who are you, and how did you find this place? Are you now or have you ever been affiliated with the Ontario Provincial Police, Royal Canadian Mounted Police, or other government entities?" he recites, a line I'm sure he's rehearsed numerous times.

"No," I say, holding my hands up and letting my gun show — pointed to the air — as I slowly start to stand up to my full height. "My name is Adrian O'Connor, former Navy SEAL. The woman with me is Rebecca Summers, former NATO and love of my life. Our car broke down a few miles east of here, and we ran into some trouble on the road. We're trying to get to the nearest town."

As I reveal myself and the man gets a full view of just how massive I am, his eyes widen. I give him a quick assessment. He might be an intimidating man himself, if I weren't around. He hasn't shaved in what looks like years, a scraggly brown beard with streaks of gray running down to his chest. He's wearing filthy blue jeans and a red plaid shirt with suspenders, and the shotgun he's holding is clearly used for hunting turkey rather than killing humans, but I suspect it would do a good job of scaring off any officials who came snooping around his property.

"Is that so?" he says, keeping the gun trained on me even as I step out into the open, to Becca's dismay. "And just what is a Yankee with a military service record doing this far north?"

"Just trying to settle down on some land of my own with the woman I love," I answer, my voice utterly calm and confident as I look him right in the eye. "Trying to leave the past behind me."

He glares at me long and hard, those icy eyes judging my case as I stand there before the grizzled old man. After a long few moments, he raises his gun, putting a hand on a hip and smirking.

"Well now, I reckon that's something I can empathize with. Call me Jones. Put that pistol away and come on in, can't have you traipsing around blind outside."

Jones heads indoors, and I smile down at Becca, who's giving me an incredulous look. "Did… did that just happen?" she whispers as she comes up to my side, and I hug her to me. "How did you know you could talk him down like that, Adrian?"

"Men like him who are Canadian-born have a thick accent you can recognize," I say simply, leading her towards the porch. "But him? I'd guess he's from somewhere around Pennsylvania. He's American."

Becca's eyes widen in understanding as I follow Jones indoors, where I see him tending to a cast-iron pot of what smells like the some kind of stew that smells better than anything I've smelled since getting back home.

"Good timing," Jones grunts, "venison's fresh. Don't have seats for three, m'afraid."

The interior of the house is about what I'd imagine. He's done a lot of woodwork by hand on the interior, setting up his own table, a cut stump as a seat, a few racks for drying herbs and salted meat, and so on. There's a crackling fireplace at the far end of the house, and the bed is covered in animal pelts, probably cured by hand. A true woodsman.

And as I glance at the table where the meat in the stew was cut up not long ago, my suspicions are confirmed — the knife laying there is unmistakably US military issue.

"Thanks, Jones," I say, standing still in the middle of the house while Becca walks around curiously, taking in the rustic sights all around her. It makes me happy to see a sparkle of pleased interest in her eyes as she looks at it all. I was worried she'd be too accustomed to city living to enjoy this kind of place.

Unfortunately, I quickly noticed there was no phone – or electricity – in his home, and I know better than to ask. Someone who wants to live off the grid doesn't want telemarketers calling at dinner, and a recluse like Jones wouldn't take kindly to someone seeming to look down on his way of living.

"I suppose it would be presumptuous to ask what brings another American like you all the way up here," I add.

"It would," Jones chuckles as he brings us a pair of hand-carved wooden bowls full of the savory stew, which Becca digs into immediately, ravenous. "But I reckon I can make an exception for a SEAL."

I glance around the place after accepting the bowl with a curt nod. "Appreciated. Sorry to spook you like that."

"Ya didn't spook me," he grunts, taking his own portion and taking a seat at the makeshift table, "I can hear something unusual coming through these woods for miles. Figured you were cops, based on how quiet you moved, but this makes a little more sense. That gun tells me you're not *just* wandering out here, though," he adds, narrowing his eyes suspiciously.

"We're on the move with a rough crowd on our tail," I admit, "but they're not woodsmen. Bikers. If they come through this neck of the woods, you'll hear them from even further than us."

He gives a thoughtful nod, and though he doesn't show it, I can sense a hint of appreciation in the warning. This old veteran isn't as well-defended as he lets himself on to be, especially against a whole crew of mobsters.

"And what'd you do to piss off that crowd?" he rumbles.

"Brought the war back home with me," I say in a low tone, glancing out the window. I see a hint of sympathy sparkle in the man's haggard eyes. He doesn't nod, but digs into his food for a few moments before speaking again.

"Figures. I get my ass all the way out here, but somehow, it always spills back over."

"You're not old enough for Korea," I comment, looking him over. "Let me guess — Vietnam?"

I see the man's hand tighten around his spoon, but he gives the faintest of nods. For a moment, as he gazes into the fire, I can see memories flashing before his eyes in the same way they flash before mine in the still of the night sometimes.

"Army," he says. Becca is watching him from across the room, her eyes full of sympathy that I know the veteran doesn't want. "Got shipped out with a handful of other teenagers like me. We were about to start college or some shit, I don't remember that well. Only one of us who knew what he was doing was our lieutenant. Sniper caught him the first hour we were out in the field."

He gives a grim smile as he looks up at me.

"See, folks like you, you're lucky. They teach *you* how to survive in the jungle for a few months with nothin' but a knife and a handful of diseases. Me, I got by on dumb luck. Guess living like this became the only thing I could do," he says ruefully, looking around at his rough living space.

"I hear that," I say after finishing off my food. Becca is still, listening to us speak about a life I'm glad she'll never have to know. "Strange as it is, traipsing around the woods like this almost feels more like home than a new house would. You get used to the wilderness."

He gives a chuckle, looking out the window. "Well, that, and staying out in the woods makes you feel less homeless than the city streets back home."

I nod, and the two of us share a silent moment together, wordlessness sometimes a better medium for our experiences than anything else. Veteran support is bad now, but it was even worse for men like Jones back in the Vietnam era. Those boys got drafted and thrust back into society without the help they needed, left to fend for themselves in a world that had moved on.

No wonder so many of them chose to live out in the wilds like this.

"Sometimes, I think about a few of my friends who deserted to Canada to dodge the draft," he muses. "Reckon a little regret that I didn't do the same is what brings me up here, to answer your question."

"When the world turns its back on you, you do what you need to to get by," I say, looking up at Becca, who's watching me with shining eyes. She's seen her share of action, I know, but she was lucky enough to get out before the scars really had a chance to take form.

"Anyhow, you say you're headed for the next town over," Jones says, standing up once we've eaten. He strides to a window on the opposite side of the cabin, and he points north. "There's a railway that runs about a mile north from here. It heads straight to Collingwood. Little town, not much to it. But if you're after civilization, that's your best bet."

Becca looks confused a moment, glancing between me and Jones. "But it doesn't stop out in the middle of the woods."

Jones chuckles, shaking his head. "No, sweetheart, it don't. Hope your man here knows how to jump. You're roughing it out here."

"I've got you covered," I say, casting a wink at Becca with a smile.

Jones glances between us with a questioning look, and I smile at him, putting my arm around Bex. He grunts and smiles, shaking his head. "You harden yourself so long, you forget what it looks like to be soft with someone," he muses at us. "But hey, you two look like you've got a good thing going on, I can tell that much. Keep each other safe out there. That's the only advice that's ever been worth its shit to me, all my life."

"Thanks, Jones," says Becca, and before long, we're heading out of the house and marching north again, not wanting to lose time.

A few minutes later, we reach a steep incline, and I'm leading the way around a rocky path over a deep ravine. It's been steady going, and we haven't said much since leaving Jones behind. Becca finally breaks the silence.

"Hey, Adrian," she says softly. "What I saw back there between you and Jones, talking about combat…"

"Yeah?"

She hesitates a moment. "I know you've got scars that go deeper than anything I could hope to understand," she says, her voice quieted yet strong. "You're stronger than I could ever be. I know I can help you when I can, but…"

I can sense her thoughts, and I glance back at her, taking her hand and giving it a gentle squeeze. "Bex, stop right there. Don't think for a second that just because you haven't been through the same hell as me that you aren't the most important thing in my life."

She opens her mouth to speak, then shuts it again, and I continue.

"It's important for trauma victims to be able to talk about their experiences," I say, "whether it's you and me or anyone else who's gone through those nightmares. But the last thing I want is for you to devalue what you are to me. You're my anchor, baby," I say, smiling, and her eyes shine with admiration.

After a few moments, she speaks. "I guess I just wasn't used to seeing you so open like that," she says, but smiles. "It was nice. Adrian, I know you probably think you need to hide certain parts of you. Everyone who's seen combat has had to… to change something about themselves. Like a mask. But I just wanted to tell you I-"

There's a shift in the rocks under us, and Becca's voice is suddenly cut off. I spin around in time to see her wide eyes as the breath leaves her. Her body is falling back as the ground gives out from under her, and below her is nothing but dozens of feet of sheer rock.

My body lunges out for her, heedless of my own safety as my hand reaches out for her as I hear her cry out my name.

The world has simply disappeared from beneath my feet, and I scream in terror, feeling that the end is definitely near. My arms reach up, scrambling for something to hold onto as one of the backpacks fall down the cliff. It hits against a couple branches that jut out from the rock before hitting the ground way below.

My feet are scraping at the almost sheer decline of the rocky bluff, chipping off tiny chunks of rock and clay as I flounder for a foothold or handhold. In one violent instant, I learn what it feels like to have your entire life play out before your eyes like some kind of shoddily edited, staccato-frame film reel.

Running along the babbling creek as a child, a long stick in my hands dragging the surface of the clear water. Lying in bed watching the frightening shapes of tree branch shadows waving and swaying on my ceiling during a thunderstorm. Walking across the stage at my high school graduation ceremony, the stiff toe of my dress shoes catching on a warp in the wood and causing me to stumble in front of the whole congregation. Laughing with my college friends at three in the morning in my little, cramped dorm room as we celebrate finally finishing our end-of-year exams. Staring out the tiny window of a helicopter as I'm flown over the desert, my stomach twisting and turning with anxiety and anticipation. The first time I saw Adrian's bright green eyes from across that crowded bazaar in Afghanistan, when my heart skipped a beat and my body flushed hot, then cold, then hot again.

The sensation of holding my newborn daughter in my arms for the first time, when I was drenched in sweat and so exhausted I could barely speak. Maya's pink little face blinking up at me with wonder in her wide, beautiful eyes.

Adrian standing in the doorway of my hotel room in Mississauga just days ago, an overwhelming, yet indescribable tidal wave of emotion lapping between us even as we stared at each other without words. The memory of being swept into his arms, the undeniable feeling of coming home.

And it's all over, isn't it?

I'm falling into the steep ravine.

But just when I'm beginning to accept that I'm a goner, two powerful hands wrap themselves around my wrists tightly, a vice grip that feels both shocking and familiar at the same time. I glance upward to see that Adrian has grasped hold of my arms, the expression on his face horrified and determined in equal measure.

"Don't let go!" he shouts, starting to hoist me up. "I've got you, Bex!"

Still in a daze, I watch as he pulls me up from an otherwise imminent death or at least severe injury, lifting me gently as though I weigh nothing at all. His strength and ability to remain calm and focused in such a harrowing situation surprise me still. As he tugs me up over the brink of the ledge, I collapse on top of him, trembling and breathless. Adrian throws his arms around me and pulls me close to his chest, covering the top of my head with fervent kisses.

"You… you saved me," I gasp, tears choking my throat.

"God, Becca, I could have almost lost you. I thought I was going to watch you die," Adrian whispers, pulling me up to cup my cheeks and stare intently into my face. His jaw is tensing and his eyes are fierce, vivid green, and intense with emotion. "You mean more to me than anything, and I almost watched you disappear."

"I'm sorry," I cried, my voice breaking over the syllables as I fold into his touch. "The bag. The guns you took, they were all in there," I whimper.

His thumb finds my jaw and he looks seriously into my eyes.

"We'll be okay, Bex. I have my pistol still, and my

blade. And we're going to call for help once we find a phone. We'll make it through."

My body is shaking and cold, shivering with the fear of such a close call. Adrian kisses me passionately on the lips, his tongue pushing into his mouth as his fingers course down my jaw, my neck, my shoulders. When we finally break apart to take a deep breath, my chest is heaving and tears are rolling down my cheeks. I can't believe I'm alive. It's all thanks to this beautiful, powerful man that I am even around to keep breathing the sweet country air.

"Let's get moving," he suggests, helping me up to my feet. I'm still a little wobbly, my legs trembling and my stomach churning. But the breeze and the beaming sun have never felt so magical on my skin. I've never tasted such heavenly air sucked into my lungs. The lush green forest around us seems to teem with pulsating, enthusiastic life, like I can feel the very heartbeat of the wilderness pumping all around me with every springy step. I've never felt more mystical and exhilarated as I do now, having barely escaped an awful fate.

"So, I hope you're planning to stick around. Who knows what might have happened to me by now if I didn't have you to look out for me," I tell Adrian, falling in step beside him. He takes my hand and kisses it, holding my palm to his stubbly cheek for a moment as though to breathe in my scent.

"It's my fault that we're in this mess in the first

place, so it's only fair that I keep you from falling into any other traps. I got you into this and I plan on getting both of us out alive and unscathed," he declares firmly.

I smile up at him. "I have no doubt in you. I believe in you completely, Adrian."

"And you… Becca, I can't imagine my life without you in it. I refuse to live in a world empty of your beauty and spark. You make me feel things I never thought I would be able to feel again. After everything I saw, everything I did, when I was a soldier… well, let's just say I felt like I didn't deserve happiness. Or love. But you have opened my eyes. For the first time, I feel hopeful. Like there is a future waiting for me beyond my years of service. These hands can do something other than destroy things—they can hold you. They can touch you and bring you joy," he says tenderly, pulling me close as we walk through the woods toward what looks like a dreamy clearing in the middle of the trees.

"Oh, your hands definitely bring me joy," I remark cheekily, and Adrian laughs. He reaches around to slap my ass and I let out a little giggle, pretending to run away from him. He comes bolting after me and tackles me to the ground, expertly wrapping his arms around me so that his arms cushion my fall completely. We roll together in the dewy moss and tiny flowers like two rambunctious kids, carefree and totally absorbed with love.

Adrian straddles me and leans down to press his lips against mine, his thigh shoved between my legs so that I can feel his cock hardening against my pelvis. I arch upward toward that stiff rod, rubbing against it so that I elicit a deep, appreciative groan from Adrian's throat. My whole body thrills at the vibration of his hums and moans, and I can feel myself getting wet between my thighs.

Adrian looks up for a moment and does a double take, then grins widely.

"What is it?" I ask, a little breathlessly. It's hard for me to focus on anything at the moment except for the sensation of Adrian's shaft hard on my body.

"We found the railroad tracks," he replies, pointing over my head. I tilt my head backwards to see the dark, heavy metal rails peeking out several yards away from a patch of overgrown weeds.

"Good for us," I comment, reaching up to pull Adrian back down to me. I don't know if it's just the usual animalistic attraction I feel for him, or if my brush with death has ignited a new, adrenaline-fueled spark of desire within me, but suddenly nothing in the world matters to me but my need to feel Adrian close. To feel him inside me.

Without missing a beat, Adrian tears off my shirt. I kick off my shoes and he pulls my denim shorts down my legs and drops them to the side, then hooks a finger under the hem of my panties to yank them back, leaving my wet cunt exposed to the country air. I inhale sharply as he begins to flick his fingertips along my damp slit, his thumb tracing gentle circles around that tight bud of nerves so that I'm moaning and crying out for release. But I don't want to give it up just yet— I want to feel Adrian inside me when I come.

"Please, Adrian," I beg softly. "Please. I need you."

"Whatever you say, baby girl," he growls, unzipping his pants to let his enormous cock spring free and rub against my ready, aching hole. I buck against him, urging him to fuck me — now. As he pushes inside of me, I moan and clench around his swollen shaft, feeling so full and complete yet again. Adrian makes me feel like I'm a whole person again, like nothing up until now has really shown me true contentedness, nothing like what he does to me when we're pressed close together like this.

"I saw my life flash before my eyes," I whisper as Adrian begins to thrust with forceful, nearly violent movements, like he wants to use me. Like he could easily break me into pieces. "And nothing made me so sad to leave this world as the thought of being without you," I finish, as my climax builds and builds.

"I can't believe I nearly lost you," he replies, his breathing rough and ragged at my ear. I bury my face in his warm neck and press a nipping kiss into the soft flesh there so that Adrian groans and fucks me even faster. He's slamming into me now, striking my g-spot like a battering ram until I'm crying out and grasping at him, my body pulsating with overwhelming shocks of ecstasy. I can feel the walls of my cunt twitching around Adrian's cock, squeezing his hard length, bringing him close to the edge, too.

There's a loud, nearly deafening sound as the ground begins to rumble and shake beneath us, and I realize — vaguely, with some distant part of my brain — that the train is approaching! But I can't bear to rip myself away from Adrian yet, not now. My legs are still wrapped tightly around his waist as he fucks me with wild abandon, his cock spearing me with every violent thrust. Finally, his hands ball into fists on either side of me and he's gasping for breath.

"Oh god, fuck!" he cries out. "You feel so good, Becca!"

"Give it to me," I plead, "fill me up!"

"Fuck... Bex," Adrian groans, and just as the ground starts to vibrate more intensely with the approach of the train, he releases a thick, hot stream of seed deep inside my clenching cunt. We barely have time to take a breath before Adrian hops to his feet, zips up his pants, and helps me hurriedly put on my clothes. The train is within sight now and we need to dive into the bushes so we aren't spotted by the conductor or any passengers before we find a railway car to jump onto. Adrian takes me in his arms and we roll into a rough patch of underbrush to watch the train rolling toward the clearing. The sound of the horn blowing and the screech of metal on metal makes my head ache and my vision swim. I've never been so close to a train before — well, without being *inside* the train, of course. I realize with a sinking feeling just how difficult it will be to jump that high and fast onto a railway car. It is a feat of athleticism and grace I don't know if I can pull off properly, and if I don't make it, the results will undoubtedly be deadly.

How has my life turned into one harrowing near death experience after another?!

But before I get the chance to ruminate further on the chances I might actually die attempting this maneuver, Adrian takes my hand and dashes out of the bushes, yelling, "GO!"

He takes one flawless, almost gazelle-like leap and lands on the side of a brick-red car, but in the process, his hand lets go of mine to grasp the side. I know in this split second my only chance of survival is to follow suit — I have to jump.

And so I do, but to my horror I am nowhere near as graceful or strong as Adrian. I leap forward and immediately begin to slide down the side of the railway car, my fingernails digging into the chipped red paint as my feet scramble for a foothold. I get a dizzying flash of deja vu, as once again Adrian has to reach out and swing an arm around me to yank me upward to relative safety, but the first time, he misses.

I slide further down the side of the car, my toes barely locked onto the little ledge of wooden moldings beneath me. Adrian quickly and nimbly shimmies along the side to jump into the opening, full of what smells like coal and hay. He is attempting to get in a better, more stable position before reaching out to give me a hand, and I look forward to see that there is a thick tree branch poking out from the woods, directly in line with where my body will be hanging off the side of the train in less than thirty seconds.

Adrian flings a hand out to me, just a couple feet to my left, shouting, "You have to jump! Trust me! Jump and take my hand!"

The weight of Becca's body as I grasp her hand feels like nothing as adrenaline rushes through my body. I wrap my hand firmly around her wrist as she gets a hold of mine, a deep ravine below the train now passing under us, and I haul her up onto the train car with a grunt, just before a sharp tree branch splinters violently against the side of the car.

She melts into my arms once she's up, hugging me tightly and shivering while I move her away from the car's entrance, the rhythmic rumbling of the train's motion all around us. I brush her hair out of her eyes and kiss her deeply, and she sighs into it, a moan that at once savors my touch and revels in the relief of being once again safely in my arms.

"I don't think most train travelers go through

that every time," she breathes when our kiss breaks, a lopsided grin on her face.

"No, but most travelers don't get caught having as much fun as we do," I say, holding her chin in my fingers to watch her eyes sparkle up at me in admiration.

I've had people put their trust in me, but with Becca, it feels all the more right, like a glove that's a perfect fit. Every moment I get to protect her feels fulfilling in a way I never even knew in the SEAL service.

Becca turns to take a few cautious steps toward the huge sliding door of our train car, glancing out at the wilderness below us. The ravine she nearly fell into was deep and deadly, but it was also thankfully short. Before long, the train is back into the woods, and there's greenery all around us, the sweet smells of the forest filtering into our car.

I step up beside her and put a hand on her shoulder, stroking it reassuringly. "Just a smooth ride back to town from here. You should get some rest and enjoy the ride. It's probably going to be a while."

"Suppose a train car is better than the forest floor again," she jokes, making her way over to a corner of the train and taking a seat, setting her backpack to her side and pulling out her blanket to start wrapping it around herself. "Do you think we'll get in trouble for being out here like this? In the train car, I mean?"

"I'd like to see someone try to tell us off for it," I laugh, "but I don't think your average hitchhiker like us is fleeing from a bunch of murderous Russian hitmen."

She looks a little less amused by the statement than I'd intended, so I come to take a seat beside her, my huge form getting slowly to the ground and pulling her in tight beside me.

"Hey, don't worry, Bex," I say, my voice low. She leans into me, resting her head on my shoulder silently. "I don't know who all they've got out there looking for us, but as long as I'm here, they're going to have more on their plate than they can handle."

She nods, silent a few moments. "There was something really peaceful about that guy we met back there in the house. Jones. I don't know what it was, but even if it was all kind of rough around the edges, there's something… I guess 'quiet' is the word for it."

I nod, understanding her meaning perfectly, and I feel a swelling of pride in my chest as she says it. "That's a good way of putting it. Long way away from all the noise of the city. Everything that comes with it."

"I've never really been much more than a city girl at the end of the day," she says, snuggling in closer to me, "but with you at my side out there, I feel so protected, you know? Like there's nothing out there that could really hurt me, even though we're so far away from everything."

"The wilderness has a lot more dangers than it lets on," I say, feeling her relaxing more and more with the steady, rhythmic bumping beneath us. "It's not made for mankind. We haven't tamed it, ripped it up and remade it how we like it. There's a level of give and take you have to consider when living out there."

"I don't know about any of that," she admits as I take her hand in mine and plant a kiss on her head.

"I can teach you," I say, and she looks up at me curiously.

"Oh yeah?"

"Yeah," I grin back down. "Teach you what herbs are good to keep and which are toxic, how to track wild game, how to tend livestock…"

I notice the intimidated look on her face, and I chuckle, giving her a reassuring squeeze. "Maybe we'll just start with building a campfire."

"No, no, I want to learn," she says, her sparkling smile warming my heart as she sits up a little. "It's just a little overwhelming, how much I'm gonna have to change. But there's nobody I'd want to make that change with besides you, Adrian."

We look into each other's eyes, silent for a few moments, just enjoying the quiet company of one another along with the uncomplicated background noise around us. The rustling of the trees almost has a rhythm to it as the train engine rumbles along, and I feel truly peaceful for the first time in a long time.

For a half-hour, that spell of peace holds both of us entranced, warm and secure in each other's embrace as Becca gets lulled into a peaceful sleep by the train, and I listen to the world around us.

It's only a few minutes after Becca's fallen to sweet sleep that my ears prick at something unusual.

I glance out the door, furrowing my eyebrows. The sound of the train is the same as always, chugging along at an even pace along the tracks. Why did I just think I heard something different? It was another rumbling, steady sound, but it wasn't quite what we'd been enjoying the past few moments.

Then I hear the noise more distinctly outside — the revving of accelerating engines. Motorcycle engines.

"Becca, get up," I say immediately, springing to my feet. Becca awakes with a yelp, startled, but this isn't the time for gentle awakenings. I need to get her moving. *Now.*

"What?! What is it?" she says blearily, but her eyes quickly alight with attentiveness as they meet the concern in my gaze and see me pulling out my pistol, checking the magazine and readying it.

"We have company," I say, looking out door and clenching my jaw. The train has taken us alongside the highway, forest giving way to farmland, and now

I can hear the sounds of motorbikes rapidly approaching us.

And there are a lot of them.

"Oh my god," Becca gasps, hearing the sound too, "how did they find us?" I don't give a response. I know the most likely answer is that they tracked us to Jones's cabin and interrogated him for our whereabouts. I curse myself. I knew leaving him behind alive wasn't a good idea. My training would have had me silence him to ensure our safety, but I was still fighting the monster I left behind in the service — do I really have to become so ruthless to preserve our safety?

It might be too late.

"Get onto the roof," I say calmly, as evenly as I might have given instructions to civilians before a firefight really got bloody. "Keep your body as low as possible. They're going to be looking for cars like ours and peppering them with bullets. If you're up there, I can buy you some time while I deal with them."

"I'm not going to leave you behind!" she protests, but I kiss her deeply, wrapping my hand around the back of her neck to pull her into me before I break away and guide her toward the roof access — a small, rusting ladder with a hatch at the top of the car.

"You aren't leaving me behind, baby," I say, "I'll die before I let that happen."

She gives me a longing look full of desire, but she swallows the sob coming to her throat and nods, turning and climbing up the ladder.

Not a moment too late, either. No sooner is Becca pushing herself flat against the rooftop than I hear a shotgun blast hit one of the cars behind us. There are other cargo cars that could accommodate people, so it sounds like I was right — they're spraying each with bullets in an attempt at flushing us out.

At least they won't be looking at the car roofs, then. I pray there's no one else around that could get injured.

I hear nearly a dozen bikes roaring up alongside us, though, and I realize I'm going to need to think on my feet for this. All I have is six rounds and my combat knife, and the knowledge that Becca's life is on the line.

I really ought to let the bikers take a few shots at me to even the odds.

Thinking back to how the bikers approached us the first time they struck, I made a mental note of where to strike first. Because as soon as I reveal myself, I'm going to have about a second before I'm riddled with bullets.

I whip around from the cover of the metal door and see just what's coming my way, my pistol at the ready. In a split second, I see what I thought I'd heard — about a half dozen motorcycles roaring forward, guns aimed at the car they're passing. And I'm sure there's another half dozen on the other side of the train. Before the ones in the lead have a chance to react to my presence, I act.

My pistol fires two rounds, and two men die before they know what hit them. The leaders of the pack fall, and their bikes go with them, spinning out of control to the now-alarmed mobsters that were following. As the vehicles careen to a crash, they take out two more of the pack, sending men screaming to the ground as they hit the dirt before their own bikes roll over them and crush them.

I pull myself back into the car as bullets come flying from the other two gunmen. I hear the sound of the engines roaring as they blaze forward, eager on avenging their allies, but as soon as the first of them comes within sight, I fire a round into his neck, and he chokes on his own blood as he drops his weapon, his bike veering into the train and pinning him against the side before he lets the acceleration go and falls to the ground a mangled body.

I hardly notice the carnage under the wheels, too busy putting a bullet in the last man's head as he watches the massacre with wide eyes.

The six on the left side of the train are dealt with just as I hear the thud of boots hit the floor of the car, and I whirl around just in time to catch the fist of the man who just leaped aboard.

Behind him, I see the driver of the bike that delivered him onto the train.

That makes my heart leap into my throat. If the bikers are carrying passengers, then some of them might be climbing on top of the cars. *Becca!*

No more time for fooling around. I deliver a swift strike to the man's solarplexis with my knee, making him double over before my hands wrap around his head. With a swift twist, there's a crack as I break his neck and let him fall to the ground outside in a tangled mess of a roll.

The driver who dropped him off is dumbfounded as I race towards him, putting my gun away and taking out my knife.

I leap onto the bike just as he starts to veer away, and I land right behind him, my weight nearly toppling the vehicle and making it swerve to the right, into the crowd of stupefied other bikers.

He shouts something at me in Russian, but I'm not paying attention to his words. I reach into his holster and pull out his pistol, and before those around me can react, I've fired off three rounds and taken down three bikers. Their engines sputter as they crash to the ground, and the two of them that bore passengers crush their riders under them.

Two bikes left. The driver in front of me is getting bolder in his moves to try to shake me off, so I draw my knife across his throat and let him slump forward before shoving him off the bike and taking the handles myself.

The engine roars forward as I veer off to the right, aiming for one of the bikers, who lets out a shout as I approach. He fumbles for his gun, but my knife is already out. I feel the heat of our engines as I drive the bike right up alongside him to plunge my knife into the back of his neck, and he lets out a gurgling scream before slumping down on his handlebars, the weight of his body pushing the acceleration down and sending him hurdling forward before his bike spins out of control.

I feel a searing pain on my shoulder as a bullet grazes me, and I turn my attention back to my left, where the last bike's passenger aims his gun at me. There are two on the bike, one driving, one leveling his pistol at me. I hit the brakes just before he fires, and the barrel flashes as bullets whiz in front of me.

He swears, but I cut him off with a quick shot to the head. The passenger gunman's blood sprays out onto the driver, who cries out in horror while I speed forward.

Before he can react, I cut left *hard*, and my bike connects with his. Suddenly, he's too busy trying to keep his bike from falling over to worry about me. But I'm relentless, pushing my bike further against his until he's nearly getting crushed up against the side of the moving train.

"Maniac!" he splutters as he fights to keep me

from ramming him against the train car, his thick Russian accent muffled under the train engine's sounds.

"Should have thought of that before taking this job," I spit back at him before elbowing him in the head. He loses control of his bike, and it skids to the ground as part of his body gets caught under the rolling wheels. I don't look back at the sound of a sickening crunch.

Something on top of the train as my attention.

I didn't fail to notice that one of the bikes no longer had a rider on it. As I look up to the top of the train, I get my answer as to why.

Glaring down at me with a look of vicious malice is a familiar face: the face of the Spetsnaz commander who's been haunting my nightmares for years. I feel my heart pound with fury as his visage twists into a cruel smile, and he gives a mocking salute before he disappears from sight, moving towards the front of the train.

Right where Becca was headed.

I speed over to the train car. There's no ladder leading to the top, just the metalwork that forms the structure of the car itself. I have no time to waste looking for safe access. In the breadth of a second, I stand up on the seat and handlebars of the bike and leap off it before it can slow down, and as my hands find purchase on the metalwork, I hear it crash in a ball of fire and twisted metal behind me.

My body acts like the finely tuned machine it is as I haul myself up and over the top of the train in a fluid motion, and the moment my feet touch the ground, I whip my pistol back out and point it in front of me…

…where I see my Russian friend holding Becca with an arm around her neck, his pistol pointed at her temple as both their faces look into me — one full of hatred, the other pale with fear.

"Adrian O'Connor," comes the Russian's thickly accented voice, a voice that hasn't changed a bit since we last met.

"You have me at a disadvantage," I reply, my voice barely restraining the blinding rage just under my skin as I shout over the wind that whips across our bodies atop the train.

"My name is Anatoly Bogdanov," he growls as Becca's eyes look at me pleadingly. "I was once a commander, but I resigned in shame, thanks to you."

Thanks to your bad call and arrogant pride, I think to myself, but I know that I have to measure my words carefully right now. This has just become a hostage negotiation, and I'd lay down my own life before letting Becca's go.

"What happened wasn't our fault, Anatoly," I say calmly. I need to talk him down if I can, just long enough for him to release Becca. Nothing else matters right now. "We got bad intel. Someone over our heads crossed some wires, and some good men paid the price."

"The best men!" he barks, and now I can see the pain in his eyes as he presses the cold metal against Becca's head, and she whimpers. "*My* men, O'Connor! They had families, and you killed them! My team went through everything together, but you ruined it all. The survivors went rogue after that operation. I had to lose my life's savings to bribes to cover it all up. When I left the service, I had *nothing*! Nothing but the Bratva, and the chance to take revenge."

"They ride you for all you've got, then leave you out on the streets," I say, keeping my tone level. "I know, Anatoly, I've been there. I nearly had to resign after that mission — I lost one of mine, too. My best man. My best *friend*."

"But you got to move on," he rasps, his finger on the trigger, and I feel my body tense. "You got to keep rising through the ranks, and now, you retire with a bright future and a beautiful woman."

He tightens his grip around Becca's neck, and I see her face starting to redden. He's choking her. His eyes are bloodshot, and there's a vein pulsing in his forehead.

"That's because I knew when to let it go, Anatoly!" I shout. "You can walk away from this, get in touch with the rest of your men, get some closure!"

"No," he snarls, readjusting Becca in his grasp as he poises himself to pull the trigger, tears streaming down Becca's face. "I'm going to make you taste the bitterness I've had to live with for years, and then I'm going to break your body!"

The sound of a gunshot rings out with a bang.

natoly's attention snaps to the road beside the train along with mine, and his one remaining eye widens in shock.

The old recluse called Jones is driving a beat-up old pickup truck alongside the train, and he's fired off the very same shotgun he aimed at us earlier today, getting Anatoly's attention.

Just long enough for me to act.

The moment the Russian's eyes are away from me by the sudden distraction, it's Becca who seizes the moment. She breaks away from Anatoly, twisting his wrist around behind him and making him cry out in pain before he can do so much as react.

She's trained military too, after all.

The moment she holds him still, I fire the last bullet in my weapon at his head.

Becca recoils and collapses to the ground as Anatoly's lifeless body falls away from her, onto his side, his blood streaming from the hole in his head. Dead.

I look down to Jones and give him a silent nod as he grins up at me, giving a hoot before stowing his weapon and pulling away from the train, presumably retreating to his neck of the woods once more. I don't know how he survived the bikers, and I never will — his story is his own, and I know that's the way he'll want to keep it.

I rush forward and catch Becca in my arms, who breaks down into sobbing immediately. We hug each other tight, and I feel the weight of the world off my shoulders as I pepper her face in kisses while she lets it all out.

"I thought I'd lost you," she sobs, clinging to my shirt and burying her face in my chest.

"What'd I tell you, baby?" I say, stroking her hair gently as I hold her up, letting her sink into me and breathe deeply. "As long as I'm alive, nothing's gonna get between us. And now, nothing else will ever stand a chance.

*I*t's been about a week since our fight on the train. We made it to Collingwood and got a ride back to Toronto after making a few calls with some well-informed contacts of mine.

As much as I want it to be, the fight isn't over just yet. There's one last little detail to take care of: the Bratva still has a hit out on me, even though the man who paid for it is dead.

So when Becca and I swing open the doors of the biggest Russian bar in the city, it's no surprise when a dozen sets of eyes glare at us while I strut inside.

I'm wearing a gray suit with a white, unbuttoned shirt, my military dog tags hanging from my neck so everyone on the club knows exactly who I am. Becca is at my side, wearing a short, red bodycon dress and black stilettos, her hair spilling over her shoulder in gorgeous waves, blood-red lipstick a challenge to everyone who looks at us.

I stride through the club as dull music pulses around us. It's a little classier than the gopnik garbage the low-ranking Bratva mobsters are known for. This place is an upscale joint run by the upper echelon of the country's Russian mob presence.

A massive bouncer approaches us, his ugly mug fixed in a scowl. I don't flinch, and after everything she's been through, neither does Becca.

"You've taken wrong turn," he says in broken, accented English. "You need to leave." He cracks his knuckles meaningfully as he glares at me, but I don't break my stride, heading for the bar.

"Hey!" he shouts, furrowing his thick brow, and he tries to grab for me as I pass him. Exactly what I was waiting for.

Using the brute's own weight against him, I take a hold of the wrist of the meaty hand that was reaching for me, and I twist him over my shoulder, hauling his whole mass over me and slamming him down on the ground with a thud that the whole club can hear.

A quick glance around the place tells me this guy must have been one of the toughest out on the floor, because nobody seems to be in any rush to back him up. But all eyes are on us now if they weren't already. At the far end of the bar, I see a couple of men posted at a door whisper to one another before saying something into the mic in their shirts.

With Becca at my side, I walk over to the bar, where the bartender is arching an eyebrow at me.

"Moscow mule," I order.

The bartender seems mildly surprised, but nonetheless he starts mixing my drink. "You're making a terrible mistake, American," he says in a mild tone as he pours the vodka and ginger beer over ice in a copper mug. "So I'll make your last drink a double, how about that?"

I grin at him. Didn't think I'd find a barkeep with a sense of humor in a place like this. "Much obliged,"

I thank him, putting a $50 on the counter. "Now tell me — is Vitaly around? I'd like to have a chat."

"Oh, he's around," the bartender laughs as that door towards the back opens, and six burly men with guns in their hands make their way out onto the floor. I notice that most of the patrons seem keenly interested in their own drinks. I turn around and lean on the bar, smiling at the men casually. "And I believe you've just made the VIP list," the bartender adds as I down my drink.

"Here I was starting to doubt Russian hospitality," I say, setting the empty mug on the counter before approaching the group of mobsters with my arms open. The men glare at me, clearly on edge. "No need to be tense, boys, I'll come quietly."

"They really know how to treat you around here," Becca muses, walking close by my side. The Russians don't say a word, but one of them motions for me to follow with a nod toward the back door and a grunt.

We're led down a long hallway, three men in front of us, three in the back. The hallway looks designed to withstand a firefight, a long and narrow chokepoint that would be easy to defend. The owner of this place certainly knows what he's doing.

The room we're escorted into is large, dark, and overcast with a pall of cigarette smoke that makes the other few armed guards standing in the corners seem hazy. There's a huge desk in the center of the room, and I instantly recognize the man sitting at it with his hands steepled atop it.

His icy-blue eyes are glaring at me, and the darkness of the room doesn't do anything to conceal the silvery hair on his head.

"Vitaly," I greet him, "good to see you again."

"I spend thousands tracking you down for my good friend Anatoly," he says, leaning back in his chair and crossing his legs as the guards take positions around us. I can't help but notice they haven't put their guns away.

"You wipe out a strike team of twelve bikes and nearly twice as many men," he goes on, raising his eyebrows as he mentally goes over the figures, "you leave the huge mess out there in the wilderness, so my men's deaths are plastered all over the media, you *kill* my underboss Anatoly, and just as I'm about to call in some of my best international hitmen to wipe you off the face of the earth and send your body back to Anatoly's relatives, you present yourself at my doorstep."

Vitaly picks up the glass of vodka on the table, taking a drink as he watches me with even eyes. "I'd call you a strange man, Adrian O'Connor, but to tell you the truth, you remind me of myself when I was younger."

"I live to please," I say in a mocking tone, putting a hand to my chest with a smile.

Vitaly turns his icy eyes to Becca, looking her up and down. There's a flash of something in his eyes, similar to recognition, but not quite. I can't put my finger on it, but he seems to soften at the sight of my raven haired girl.

"So I get to meet the woman for whom nearly two dozen of my men are dead. She's even lovelier than I remember."

"They say looks can kill," Becca says with a wink, and the fire in her makes my chest swell with pride. Vitaly conceals a smirk. He likes a spitfire too, I suppose.

Finally, Vitaly stands up, folding his hands behind his back and pacing about the room thoughtfully. "Anatoly was a good man," he muses, "and a powerful one at that. Moreover, he was one of us. A made man of the Bratva. My very own underboss."

We lock eyes for a few long moments. I know what he's thinking. Anatoly was unstable, he was vengeful, and he was a threat to Vitaly's power. He was a threat to business, and if I had been killed in that firefight like Anatoly wanted, it's likely that a fight with Vitaly would have been next on the list in a bid for power — those international hitmen would have been for Vitaly's protection instead.

But Vitaly cannot simply shame Anatoly's memory right here in front of all his men and discuss such things openly. Then again, neither can he request a private audience. Because he knows that if I get him alone, I'll kill him with my bare hands. So instead, I must use a different approach.

"What Anatoly and I had was purely personal, you know that. He and I fought viciously in Syria, and we finished our battles here in Canada. It was over a bad call our superiors made long ago, and good men died on both sides as a result. Our fight never should have happened in the first place."

I flex my fist. "I tried to talk him down. I really did. And if I'd had my way, he'd be standing here before you instead of me."

"Yet here you are," Vitaly points out, his eyes narrowing.

"Here I am," I say, crossing my arms and looking at him firmly. "You've lost a lot of men over this too, Vitaly. A lot of men who might have had promising careers ahead of them. You can blame me if you want — I won't fault you for that. It wouldn't be the first time I got blamed for deaths that were outside of my hands."

He chuckles, but I continue. "But you and I both know that Anatoly is the reason we're standing here, and Anatoly is the reason that all those men lost their lives. And now Anatoly is dead."

"So," he says, leaning on the back of his chair with an arched brow, smiling a cool, cold smile, "you mean to propose a truce? Say that no more of my men need to die, and you and your woman can just walk away from this while we all forget it happened?

That's very bold of you, Adrian O'Connor. But then again, they only choose the bold ones for SEAL service, isn't that right?"

"You're a smart man, Vitaly," I say, glancing around at the men around us. I know that they're the real bargaining chip on the table — Vitaly's ego against my ability to kill a room full of armed guards. The odds are better than I'm used to. "I doubt you ever believed in Anatoly's little vanity project of killing me. Nobody's going to mourn my passing if I die, nobody's going to shift around big lumps of money, and nobody's going to be *really* happy about my death but one dead man's ghost."

Vitaly's face is still, his gaze hard to read through the darkness and thick smoke. But the fact that he isn't smiling tells me he's at least listening to what I have to say.

"Not many men like yourself would plead the worthlessness of their lives," he says smoothly.

"Not many men have the same things to live for as I do," I say, wrapping a strong arm around Bex and drawing her close to me. She puts a hand on my chest, leaning into me. After all this time, after everything we've been through, I realize that she trusts me more than anyone else in the world.

She trusts me to protect her. She trusts me with her life. And just as importantly, she trusts me to be the father of her child, the father that little Maya deserves. I feel utterly invincible as I hold her against me in that moment, and I can feel her smiling up at me, full of love and animalistic desire.

Vitaly looks evenly at us before standing upright again, glancing around at his men, who look back at him as if awaiting orders.

"You make a bold case, O'Connor," he admits. "But tell me this — what exactly is stopping me from simply… having you executed right here? Gun you *and* your lover down in this very office, end the blood feud in all of about ten seconds, nobody to save you but yourself?"

I smile right back at him.

"I'd like to see you try."

"I do."

The words flow into my ears and surround my whole body with welcoming warmth. I'm smiling so wide that my cheeks almost ache from the exertion. My feet feel like they're hovering several inches above the ground and my heart is so full it could nearly burst into confetti. I take a long, deep breath, feeling my tightly-tailored white dress clench around my waist as I breathe.

I'm wearing the wedding dress of my dreams: long, flowing, decorated with intricate ivory lace and netting over the skirt, with detailed pearl beading and lacing up the fitted corset top. The plunging sweetheart neckline perfectly shows off my ample cleavage, as well as the gorgeous rose quartz-and-white gold necklace my new husband's father gave me as an engagement gift. My hair is coiled behind my head in a half-up, half-down style, two thick, shining braids wrapping around to meet in a complex knot at the nape of my neck while the rest of my hair falls in loose, dark waves around my shoulders.

To my delight, as it turns out, one of my new sisters-in-law is a fantastic hairdresser, and the other is a wonderful makeup artist, so I was able to bond with two of my new family members and get my wedding look arranged at the same time. Haley and Jenny are their names, and I am overjoyed to finally have some sisters — who are already turning into the best aunties I could ever have dreamed of for my little girl. And Adrian's three older brothers, Michael, David, and Frank, are all exactly what I expected: tall, broad-shouldered, athletic good ole boys who love nothing better than backyard barbecues and an impromptu game of football. Even though they are physically intimidating and tough, the three of them treat Maya like a little princess, and she has so much fun playing with her new little cousins-in-law, who are six and eight years old, respectively.

Maya is being held off to one side in my mother's arms as my parents look on with shining, tearful eyes and bright smiles. They are both so happy to see me happy — and even though I was initially a little nervous to have my parents meet the tough, somewhat cocky father of my child, the three of them actually get along quite well. Adrian and my father bond over their shared love of the great outdoors, and my mom loves to watch Maya interact with her long-lost daddy.

In addition to gaining such a gigantic, welcoming extension to our little family, I have been most moved and overjoyed about Maya finally getting to meet Adrian. From the very first moment he held our tiny daughter in his strong, muscular arms, I could see just how very smitten he is with her. At first, she was understandably shocked to have this new man in her life — after all, Adrian is a far cry from my solemn but sweet elderly father. But within a few days, Maya was already totally warmed up to him, even calling him *da-da* without any prompting from the adults. Adrian carries her around in his arms so much that I sometimes have to gently remind him that she's supposed to be learning how to walk on her own, and that carrying her too much might stunt her development in that area.

It's like he never, ever wants to put her down. In fact, when I first half-jokingly told him that we're supposed to be helping her learn how to walk, he replied, "I know, I know. But it's like… I've gone so long feeling like my arms were empty. Like I was missing something so precious that I just couldn't put my finger on, and now… I have it. I have my little girl. And it's just so hard to let her go some-times because deep down I just can't believe she's here with me. It all seems like a dream, too good to be true."

Yes, Adrian and Maya adore each other already, and it warms my heart to see them together. For once, after years of struggling and feeling incomplete, I'm beginning to feel like I have everything I could ever want. Everything is right with the world. Adrian took care of our little mob problem, and since then all has been smooth sailing.

And now we're all gathered into this beautiful wooden mountain lodge in the Ontario countryside overlooking a lush, green valley, so that Adrian and I can make it truly official. I have said my vows, and Adrian has said his, and now the minister is about to say the words I have been dreaming of for so long.

"I now pronounce you man and wife. You may kiss the bride," he recites, beaming at us proudly. He is an old friend of the family, and I know he is probably just as moved as the rest of us.

I turn and lock eyes with my gorgeous, handsome husband, and once again my breath catches in my throat. It's so hard to believe how lucky I am to have found him again. This is everything I have ever longed for — and it's mine. At last.

Adrian wraps his arms around me, pulling me in for a passionate kiss, full of emotions neither of us could ever hope to name or describe, but what feels like a welcome home. Like we've both finally found the place we truly belong — in each other's arms.

The congregation of family and friends all cry out and applaud with joy, watching us embrace each other in this beautiful place, with the misty mountains a gorgeous backdrop behind us. Adrian leans in to whisper in my ear, and his warm breath sends a delicious shiver down my spine.

"I love you, Bex. More than anything. I can't believe you're finally mine."

I kiss him again, fervently, my hands finding his as we walk back down the aisle through a shower of confetti and flower petals. We all head out into the vast green estate for the reception, which is lit with hanging lanterns and string lights, to look like some kind of magical forest fairy party. Adrian and I cut the cake, with the help of our little daughter, and then the drinks and music begin. Everyone crowds out onto the grassy dance floor in a rush of joy, singing along and swinging around. Adrian and I can't keep our hands off of each other as we spin in circles on the dancefloor, gazing into each other's eyes. As much as I love the carefree togetherness vibe of the reception party, there is a bigger part of me that cannot wait for the night to be over… so I can finally be alone with my new husband.

Finally, around midnight, the festivities slow to a halt and the guests say their exhausted congratulations and goodbyes to head back to their respective rooms for the night in this mountain chalet we've rented. Adrian and I quietly rush upstairs to our suite, which is on the top floor, with a balcony over-looking the breathtaking scenery of the landscape.

As soon as the door shuts behind us, Adrian's lips are on mine, kissing me so needfully that I almost want to do it right here on the floor. But instead, Adrian scoops me up into his strong arms, causing me to yelp in surprise. "Where are you taking me?" I giggle.

"To bed, my little wife," he replies, kissing me on the cheek. He cradles me down onto the plush, king-sized four poster bed and starts to undress out of his multiple layers.

"I love seeing you in a tux," I purr, sitting up to watch him. "But god, do I love even more watching you take it all off."

"You're next," he growls, smirking at me as he shrugs out of his designer jacket.

I stand up and strip out of the gorgeous bridal gown, revealing the lacy white lingerie underneath, which I picked out specifically as a wedding night surprise. As soon as Adrian's green eyes land on me, his mouth falls open in disbelief.

"God, you're beautiful," he breathes, stepping closer to kiss me again. His hands roam down my shoulders to caress my breasts through the lacy fabric. The sensation of his fingers running across my nipples through the lace makes me tremble and lean into his touch. I want him so badly. Adrian quickly takes off the rest of his clothes and stands before me stark naked, his enormous cock jutting out like a spear between us. I can't help it — I fall to my knees and take him into my mouth greedily, my tongue trailing up and down the underside of his sensitive shaft until he's groaning, his fingers tangling in my hair.

"Fuck, Bex, that feels so damn good," he moans, thrusting gently into my mouth until the tip of his cock brushes the back of my throat, almost making me gag. But I want more — always more. Before I can go any further, though, he stops me and throws me onto the bed, then leans over to unclasp my garter and bustier, causing them to fall away and leave my body exposed.

He sucks in a deep breath before diving in between my thighs, his tongue lapping at my juices and suckling at my clit until I'm crying out and grasping at the sheets. He slides a finger inside of me and strokes expertly at my g-spot, and it only takes another few moments before I'm coming in his mouth, my pussy clenching around his finger.

"Ohhhh, Adrian!" I cry out desperately, over-whelmed with ecstasy. He stands up and wipes his mouth before bending down to kiss me.

"You taste like heaven," he murmurs, his hands sliding over my breasts and tweaking my nipples, sending little spirals of pleasure down my body. He knows just how to play me, every miniscule touch and breath bringing me ever closer to yet another orgasm. It's like we just fit together. Perfectly.

"I want you inside me," I mumble. "Please. Mark me as your own. I belong to you now, mind, body, and soul."

And it's like I've thrown kerosene onto an already blazing fire, because the very next moment, Adrian is pushing his massive cock inside my aching cunt, thrusting into me with abandon. "I've wanted to make you mine for so long, Becca," he whispers raggedly, leaning down to kiss me. He strikes that deep, dark spot within me again and again until I'm screaming with another climax, clutching at his back as I wrap my legs around his waist, wanting to be as close to him as possible. I never want him to let me go. This is where I belong, right here, with him.

He fucks me mercilessly, until there are tears in my eyes, until I can no longer speak coherent words, the two of us moving in perfect, relentless harmony together, back and forth. Finally, we both cry out as we come at the precise same time, Adrian shooting his virile seed deep inside me as my pussy clenches around his cock. We cling together for a moment, breathing heavily, too in love and overwhelmed to even move. Finally, Adrian collapses next to me and kisses my cheek, stroking my hair tenderly. He stares at me with a wistful smile on his handsome face, shaking his head as though he can't believe his good luck.

"This is more than I could ever dream of," he says softly. I snuggle into his arms and kiss his bare, muscular chest. "It's so hard, though, Bex. Every time I look at you it's all I can do to keep from fucking you and putting another baby inside of you."

I giggle and bit my lip, looking up at him with my heart so full it could explode in my chest. He furrows his brow at me and asks, "What? What is it?"

Here it is. The moment I have been waiting for. It's been so hard to keep it a secret, and now the time has finally come…

"Adrian, you already have," I tell him excitedly, trying to remain calm and even-toned. He nods.

"Yeah, I know. Maya," he says, looking at me funny.

I laugh and sit up, bending down to kiss him on the lips before going on, "No. I mean you've done it again. Adrian… I'm pregnant."

The joy in his eyes is almost enough to make me burst into tears. Adrian sits up and wraps me in his arms, covering my face with kisses. "I can't believe it! We're having another baby?!" he laughs.

I nod vigorously, almost too overwhelmed with feeling to even speak.

"God, Bex. I love you. I love you so much. And I love our little family. I can't wait to spend the rest of my life with you, darling," he gushes, his usual cock-sure attitude pushed aside for a moment. And when he holds me in his arms and we start to talk about the future, I know in my heart that this is what I have been waiting for all my life. This is my fairytale. This is my happy ending.

❦

Thank you so much for reading! I hope you enjoyed <3 If you have a moment, please leave a review. Other readers are dying to know what you thought.

I have plenty more bad boy romance for you, so make sure you check out my other books on the next couple of pages, and sign up for my newsletter to be notified when I have a new release on the way!

~Alexis Abbott

Killing For Her

Abducted

Stepbrothers:

Ruthless

Criminal

Standalones:

Betting on Love

Hunter's Baby

I Hired A Hitman

Vegas Boss

Rock Hard Bodyguard

Innocence For Sale: Jane

Redeeming Viktor

<u>Romance:</u>

Falling for her Boss (Novella)

Most Wanted: Lilly (Novella)

Bound as the World Burns (SFF)

<u>Erotic Thriller:</u>

The Dangerous Men Series:

The Narrow Path

Strayed from the Path

Path to Ruin

ABOUT THE AUTHOR

Alexis Abbott is a Wall Street Journal & USA Today bestselling author who writes about bad boys protecting their girls! Pick up her books today if you can't resist a bad boy who is a good man, and find yourself transported with super steamy sex, gritty suspense, and lots of romance.

She lives in beautiful St. John's, NL, Canada with her amazing husband.

facebook.com/abbottauthor

twitter.com/abbottauthor

instagram.com/alexisabbottauthor

bookbub.com/authors/alexis-abbott

pinterest.com/badboyromance

youtube.com/AlexisAbbott

ACKNOWLEDGMENTS

Thank you to my amazing Patrons. I'm constantly humbled and grateful for your support.

Ramona Cabrera
Melissa Hedrick
Virginia Swanson
Dawn Daughenbaugh
Don Doss
Stacie Currie

If you'd like to join them — and get my ebooks or paperbacks — you can find me here on Patreon.
https://www.patreon.com/alexisabbott